Home Is with Our Family

BLACK PIONEERS

⁂ JOYCE HANSEN ⁂

Home Is with Our Family

Illustrated by
E. B. LEWIS

  JUMP AT THE SUN BOOKS ✦ NEW YORK

Printed in the United States
First Edition
10 9 8 7 6 5 4 3 2 1
V567-9638-5-10274

Library of Congress Cataloging-in-Publication Data on file
Reinforced binding
ISBN 978-0-7868-5217-8
Visit www.hyperionbooksforchildren.com

SUSTAINABLE FORESTRY INITIATIVE

Certified Fiber Sourcing

www.sfiprogram.org

THIS LABEL APPLIES TO TEXT STOCK

To my family

⊰ PROLOGUE ⊱

The New York Daily Times   March 3, 1855

A MAGNIFICENT PARK
IN THE CITY

THE CITY IS finalizing plans to tear down the wretched hovels and huts in the vermin-infested area between Fifty-ninth and 106th Streets, between Fifth and Eighth Avenues. Property owners will be paid a fair amount for their land and homes; however, most of this rocky and swampy land is occupied by the dregs of New York City.

They are squatters on the land and own nothing. With their hogs and goats they live dissolute lives, creating most of the crime in this miserable part of the city. Their shanties reek of the yellow fever, which will kill them all by this summer unless even Death recoils from entering their filthy abodes.

There is one spot, however, stretching from Eighty-second to Eighty-ninth Streets between Seventh and Eighth Avenues that offers quite a contrast to its neighbors. It is a neat little settlement called the Black Village by everyone in the area.

There are now fifty well-kept clapboard frame houses, two churches, two cemeteries, and a school. Most of the 250 residents who live there are colored, hence the name.

A small number of immigrant Irish and German families, who are also property owners, live among them. The buildings and roads that form this settlement lie west of the reservoir, along a pretty knoll where grape orchards and cedars grow. Unfortunately, this little oasis will be destroyed for the better good. A magnificent and grand park will take its place.

CHAPTER 1

TALL WITHIN

THE DAY BEGAN no differently from other Sundays in Maria Peters's life. Gazing at the whitewashed walls of Zion Church, she walked next to her older brother, Moosa, toward the fifth pew, where their family always sat.

As the Peters family sat down, their neighbor, Mrs. Hamilton, rushed in. Moosa had nicknamed her the Little Magpie because she talked so much. Today she was her usual quick-moving, excitable self, stopping at a pew on the other side of them, talking to three people Maria had never seen before. Maria thought that perhaps they were a mother, father, and daughter, and that the girl might be around her own age, or maybe older. Maria tried to look without staring and wondered why the girl wore only a shawl—not enough for the chilly March morning. The older woman wore a threadbare black cloak, and the man, muscular and stocky, wore a thick, rough pea jacket and clutched a weather-beaten slouch hat.

Since Mrs. Hamilton was a member of the church benevolent society that helped poor and needy people, Maria guessed that this was a family that needed help. They looked even poorer than many of the other people who came to the church for clothing, food, or shelter.

The girl shivered slightly, and the woman put a part of her cloak around her. Maria wanted to offer the girl her own cloak. She started to point her out to Mama, but the bells began to chime, and the deep chords of the organ filled the church. All talking ceased as the parishioners bowed their heads in silent prayer while the organ played. Maria stopped looking around and bowed her head, too.

As the choir marched from the back of the church up the center aisle to the front, everyone rose, even little ones, such as six-year-old Simon, the baby of the Peters family. Eight-year-old Diana stood next to Maria and their other sister, eleven-year-old Elizabeth. Simon stood at the end.

The choir and the congregation began to sing.

> *We gather together to ask the Lord's blessing,*
> *He chastens and hastens His will to make known,*
> *The wicked oppressing now cease from distressing,*
> *Sing praises to His Name.*
> *He forgets not His own.*

Reverend Arlington faced the choir as they stepped up

to the altar. The reverend opened his Bible, and everyone knelt, except for the elderly, who would not have been able to get up. Simon eagerly scrambled to the floor, while Diana daintily adjusted her skirt as she knelt. Elizabeth clasped her hands.

As Reverend Arlington read the opening scripture— *"How excellent is thy loving kindness, O God! Therefore the children of men put their trust under the shadow of thy wings."*—Maria felt a sense of peace. She vowed not to let her mind wander to an article she'd read in the *New York Daily Times* the day before, about the city's plan to destroy their neighborhood in order to build a park. Her parents said that it was only a rumor. She was sure that if anything were wrong, Reverend Arlington would say so.

And she tried not to think so much about her birthday next Saturday, when she'd turn thirteen years old. She planned to ask Mama and Papa to let her stop going to Sunday school like the younger children.

When he finished the scripture reading, everyone stood up, and the choir and congregation sang another hymn. This was one of Papa's favorites, and Maria enjoyed hearing his deep bass voice. Mama's voice wasn't right for singing, so she whispered through the hymn, but Elizabeth sang clearly and sweetly.

> *Come Thou almighty King,*
> *Help us Thy name to sing,*
> *Help us to praise!*
> *Father all glorious,*

O'er all victorious,
Come and reign over us,
Ancient of Days!

Maria tried to act like an adult, listening carefully as the service continued. She didn't let her mind roam during the sermon and joined in when the choir and congregation sang another hymn. A loud snore escaped Diana's mouth, and Maria gently shook her awake, but soon she fell asleep again, with her head lying on Maria's arm. Maria put her arms around her and let her rest, as Mama would have done.

Struggling mightily not to doze off herself, she heard Reverend Arlington say, "And now a word from Sojourner Truth." Maria thought she was seeing a vision dressed in white as the tall black woman stood in front of the altar of Zion Church.

Maria wondered whether she was with the other new people, but just wasn't sitting with them. "Who is she?" she whispered to Moosa.

"She's a famous abolitionist and spoke at our meeting last night." Moosa's deep-set, dark eyes shone. The woman stood straight and so tall. She wore a close white cap and a long white dress, and when she opened her mouth to speak, her deep voice resonated throughout the small church, and everything ceased. Even the little ones stopped twisting and turning in their seats. Diana and Simon both woke up. Maria was transfixed.

"I was born into slavery in Ulster County, New York,

but I was always free in my soul. I was free before the state of New York did proclaim me free in 1827. My dear mother would say to us, 'My children, there is a God, who hears and sees you.' That's your power."

Then she thundered, "You!" She pointed at all of them. "Each one of *you* has the power of God inside. You have the power to bring down the walls of slavery in the Southern states." She stopped for a moment and seemed to look at every person in the congregation. Maria thought that she was staring right through her, that she was talking to *her*, in that deep, powerful voice.

"When my own child was snatched from my arms, right here in New York, I determined to get him back, even though I didn't know where he was." Her voice rose.

"I'll have my child again." She waved her long arm and balled up her fist. "I knew God would help me, though I had not a York shilling in my hand, nor a roof over my head." She held her head so high Maria thought she was growing taller right before her eyes.

Then the woman said, *"I felt tall within—I felt as if the power of a nation was with me.* I walked from county to county. I harassed anyone who would listen. I walked to the Quakers. I walked to the constable in New Paltz. I walked to the Grand Jury. I walked to and fro—all day— to and fro, from the lawyer's place to a place found for me to stay.

"God gave me the power, and my child was brought back all the way from Alabama."

Maria imagined this tall tree of a woman, trudging

among the forests and hills and roads and towns of New York, and wished she had seen her then or known her. Perhaps she could've helped her, even walked with her for a time. *And what a wonderful thing*, Maria thought, *to walk with a female who is even taller than me.*

Sojourner Truth stared again at the congregation. "You have the power, too. We can free our brothers and sisters lost in slavery. No one can stop us. No one."

And then she sang, and Maria felt the power of God in the woman's voice.

> *I bless the Lord, I've got my seal—today and*
> >*today—*
> *To slay Goliath in the field—today and today;*
> *The good old way is a righteous way,*
> *I mean to take the kingdom in the good old way.*

When she finished, there was complete silence, as if she'd touched all of their souls. The reverend had barely completed the words of the benediction, ending the church service, when the congregation seemed to erupt.

Mama and Papa and the other adults rushed over to the woman to welcome her. Maria wanted to meet her, too, but suddenly felt shy—not a feeling she was accustomed to. What could she say to her?

She looked around instead for the new family. Maybe they were related to Sojourner Truth. She'd say hello to them and meet the girl. But she didn't see them among the groups of people. They must have left quickly, as soon as the service ended. Evidently they were not with the woman after all.

Maria had no idea, as she walked out of the church with her family, how the woman and the girl would eventually affect her life.

CHAPTER 2

A SUNDAY TREAT

MARIA FOLLOWED MOOSA around to the back of the churchyard, where the horses, wagons, and a carriage or two were parked. "Oh, Moosa, I like hearing Sojourner Truth speak."

"She speaks the truth, Maria."

"Why didn't you tell me about her before?"

Dukie, their dog, who waited for the children every Sunday, trotted behind them. Moosa untied their two horses.

"I didn't think you'd be interested."

"I am interested. When can I hear her again?"

"I don't know, Maria. She comes to the meeting sometimes, but . . ."

"Then I want to go, Moosa."

He kept his face serious, but Maria saw the playful

twinkle in his eyes. "Have you lost your senses? Mama doesn't even like me and Papa going downtown to meetings at night. Anyway, we have different speakers. She might not be there."

"Well, Mama went to the meetings when she was my age. I'll be thirteen. It could be my birthday present."

He jumped into the wagon and helped her up. "Ask them, but Mama won't want you to go. You know how nervous she is about traveling downtown, especially at night."

"I know she's nervous. Always talking about kidnappers. But I'm not a baby anymore."

The sun had warmed the bare trees and the cobblestoned walkway, melting more of the leftover snow and ice. The afternoon was even brighter and warmer than it had been in the morning. They drove around to the front of the church, and Diana and Simon scrambled into the back of the wagon. Elizabeth followed, and then Maria left her seat next to Moosa, joining her sisters and Simon in the back. Mama and Papa sat next to Moosa.

"Are we going to ride down Fifth Avenue?" Diana asked excitedly.

"Yes, take Fifth Avenue, Moosa," Elizabeth said.

"We want to see the pretty houses," Maria added.

Papa turned around, smiling at them. "Your brother is not your personal carriage driver. He'll travel any way he wants to."

"Fifth Avenue takes too long. I'm going down the east side," Moosa announced.

Elizabeth and Diana moaned. Maria smiled, knowing that Moosa was teasing them.

Elizabeth wrinkled her nose. "Oh, Moosa, it's such a beautiful day, and the east side's so smelly."

Diana made a face and held her nose.

"Okay, okay," Moosa said. "We'll go down Fifth."

They passed a cluster of small shacks, where dogs and pigs scavenged among the garbage. The land was damp and swampy, and children with thin jackets and coats and worn, turned-over boots roamed with the pigs and dogs, looking for animal bones to sell to the bone-boiling plants.

Maria waited for Mama to make her usual comment.

"I thank God every day that you and your brothers and sisters do not have to do such things, just for a little something to eat," Mama said.

Papa made his living mostly as a bootblack. It was a decent living too, providing a necessary service for the wealthy men of the city so that they didn't go home with filthy boots after walking through the dirty, muddy streets. He had regular customers at the depots of several of the street railroad lines.

In addition, Papa traded downtown at the secondhand stores on Mott Street and the Bowery. He exchanged the socks, mittens, fancy handkerchiefs, and other articles that Mama and the girls made, for items that could be sold in their family store—suspenders, razor strops, shoes, jewelry that looked like gold (but wasn't), sewing supplies, and whatever else seemed necessary or useful. He also had customers downtown for the pails of buttermilk that

Mama made. The Peters children did not have to scavenge for animal bones and rags to sell.

Once they reached Seventy-ninth Street, the land was smoother. Moosa rounded the corner on to Eighth Avenue, and they traveled down a paved street. On Eighth Avenue, they saw a horse-and-railroad car in the distance, and a group of black people waiting to board. As they passed, Maria saw the sign that read COLORED PERSONS ALLOWED.

Mama said, to no one in particular, "That's why I never ride the public cars. Those people have probably been waiting for hours for a car that will let them on."

Papa sucked his teeth. "Rather walk."

Maria held on to the wagon as Moosa swerved sharply to the right to avoid hitting a group of children dashing across the street.

"I would get on any streetcar I wanted to," Maria said, but only Elizabeth heard her over the rattling and clanking wagon.

"But suppose the conductor won't let you on?" Elizabeth asked.

"He'll let me on. I'll fight back, like that colored teacher did last year. Remember? We read her story in the newspaper. And she went to the court, and the judge said colored people could ride on any railroad car they wanted to."

"I don't like fighting."

"You have to fight sometimes, Lizzie," Maria said.

They then traveled down Eighth Avenue through a

landscape of rolling hills dotted with small farms and clusters of clapboard and frame houses. Among the homes and at the edges of the farms stood workshops that made carriages and coaches, and stores that sold them. Small industrial plants produced soap, matches, wax, and paint. They passed little grocery stores and one of the many bone-boiling plants in the area. The large brick buildings of the insane asylums, orphan asylums, homes for the elderly, and hospitals were easy to recognize. These institutions, caring for the neediest people in the city, stood out among the smaller homes and shops and ramshackle shanties.

Instead of continuing downtown on Eighth Avenue, following the railroad-car tracks, Moosa turned on Sixtieth Street, heading for Fifth Avenue. They passed a slaughterhouse and a livestock pen.

Diana held her nose. "It stinks!" she yelled.

Maria and Elizabeth put their hands over their noses.

"Stop complaining. It's not as smelly as the west side!" Moosa shouted over the rattling wagon.

The scene changed as if by magic when they passed the elegant mansions of Fifth Avenue. Maria wondered what the insides of the houses looked like. A parade of fine coaches and carriages rolled down the avenue. Only a very few wagons like the Peterses' joined the parade, and there were no poor, raggedy children scrambling around the cobblestoned streets begging or scavenging among pigs and goats.

The ladies wore bonnets trimmed with the same color lace and feathers, and long capes ballooning over the newest fashions. And there were little girls wearing fur muffs and pantalets. Nudging Elizabeth, Maria pointed to one little girl. "Even Diana couldn't get that many ruffles on her bloomers," she said.

Elizabeth smiled at her sister. "She's figuring out how she can imitate some of these fashions."

"I bet those women don't spend Saturday nights sewing," Maria said, whispering so that her mother wouldn't hear her. "That's how I want to be."

"Why, Maria? All girls like to sew."

Maria shook her head and didn't answer. *Elizabeth doesn't understand*, she said to herself.

The girls continued to watch as gentlemen strolled in their knee-length frock coats and top hats, and little boys strutted in trousers and curls. Diana seemed to be in a trance as she looked at the steady stream of the rich and the stylish moving up and down Fifth Avenue.

The elegant scene changed once they moved over to Broadway. "There's the Hippodrome," Diana said, holding on to Simon's arm. "Papa took us there last year to the circus. Remember?"

Simon bounced up and down just like Diana. "We saw the people flying!" he shouted.

As they neared Grandma Isabella's home, the narrow streets grew more crowded, teeming with men, women, and children. Vendors with pushcarts weaved through the crowded streets selling their wares. It was impossible to tell which of the children were homeless and motherless and perhaps had no choice but to live by their wits or die. They looked no different to Maria from the poor children in her neighborhood.

Two- and three-story rickety wooden houses and saloons looked as if they had just been thrown against one another. Drunks staggered in and out of alleys, and women hung out of windows.

Diana and Simon both pointed at two men, one white, the other black, trying to outdance each other. A noisy crowd of people cheered them on. Mama's back stiffened. She kept turning around, as if she could distract Diana and Simon from watching the steps of the jig. "Those people are disrespecting the Sabbath," she said. "I hope I never see you children act in such a way."

Papa put his arm around her shoulders. "They won't," he said. "They'll always hear your voice, and their legs will buckle under them."

Mama's shoulders relaxed when Moosa turned the horses onto a muddy, unpaved road. Simon and Diana craned their necks, still trying to see the dancers. Maria's eyes remained on the children she saw. She wondered how they had come to live in these dilapidated shacks on these narrow, smoky streets.

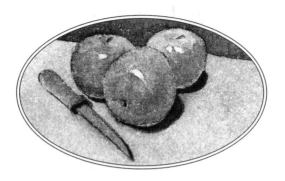

CHAPTER 3

GRANDMA ISABELLA

G RANDMA'S HOUSE, WITH its faded gray planks, stood at the very end of the unpaved street. Two wooden-frame houses sat on either side of it. These homes belonged to Grandma's two other daughters and their families. The homes sat on a half acre of land with beeches, poplars, and one large elm tree that offered shade in the summer. St. Philip's Church, which Grandma attended, was across the street. It was the church where Papa and Moosa went to the abolitionist meetings on Saturday night.

Whenever they rode up the path to Grandma's, Maria always recalled Mama's story about the New York City riots against blacks and abolitionists in 1834. She imagined Leonard Street in flames, as her mother had always described it, and Grandma Isabella standing stubbornly at her window, with a stick in her hand, refusing to take shelter. As soon as they rode up to the fence, Maria saw Grandma Isabella, small and dark, standing in the doorway. Isabella was Mama's mother, and both Mama and Diana resembled her.

Grandma's old, dim eyes turned lively when she saw them.

Simon yelled, "Grandma!" as if he hadn't seen her for months. He stood up before the wagon came to a complete stop.

"Be careful, Simon," Mama warned. "You'll fall on your head."

Simon got out, and then Diana followed him, running with outstretched arms. Elizabeth took her time climbing out of the wagon, careful not to catch the frills of her pantalets on any splinters or sharp edges.

Maria helped her. "You're dressed too fancy to be in a wagon, Lizzie. Wait till Papa buys a coach-and-four; then you can wear frilly drawers." Maria grinned at her own joke.

"One thing has nothing to do with the other," Elizabeth said, sounding hurt. "Mama told us that we must always look nice."

Maria picked up the can of buttermilk and started toward Grandma Isabella. "Some things don't go together, such as frilly underwear and wagons."

Grandma Isabella hugged and kissed each one of them, but seemed to linger a little longer with Moosa and Maria. They both had to bend down as she stood on tiptoe in order to kiss them.

"Grandma, have you shrunk?" Moosa joked.

"No, Moosa, you're just outgrowing yourself."

The kitchen was the largest room in the house. The first thing Maria noticed when she entered was the sweet, pungent scent of freshly baked gingerbread. A fire blazed in the stone fireplace, and Grandma's corncob pipe sat on the mantel. The large table that Grandpa had made so many years before stood in the center of the room.

Not long after they walked into the house, the rest of the family followed—Mama's two younger sisters, along with their husbands and children. As always, they brought food. The aunts had prepared lamb, with rice and gravy.

The sounds of Mama and her sisters talking softly mixed pleasantly with the bass voices of Papa and the uncles. Maria smiled to herself as she listened to Uncle George's laughter and the squeals of the children playing games outside. There was no better place to be on a Sunday afternoon.

Grandma handed Maria a knife and pushed the bowl of apples toward her. The flour and butter were already on the table. Maria peeled, cored, and cut up the apples as Grandma made the piecrust. Grandma took some of the flour and put it to the side. Then she rubbed butter into the rest of the flour, until she could ball it up in her hands without it falling into pieces. "How was church, Maria?"

Maria leaned across the table. "We had visitors. This tall woman who came and spoke, Grandma. She has a strange name...."

"Sojourner Truth. I have heard her speak at our meetings. She would walk to the ends of the earth speaking against slavery if she could."

I might follow her, Maria thought.

Grandma went to the abolitionists' meetings that Papa and Moosa attended. Another reason that Maria thought she should go.

"How old were you when you started going to meetings, Grandma?"

"I don't remember exactly. Perhaps a little older than you."

"Well, Mama told us that you took her to meetings when she was thirteen." Maria started peeling the last apple. "Don't you think Mama should let me go if I want to?"

Grandma stopped rolling the dough. "That's up to your mother."

Maria looked amused. "Tell Mama to let me go. You're her mother, so she has to listen to you."

Grandma chuckled. "I can't get between you and your mother. You should be worrying about school and your sewing."

Maria groaned.

"If you sew real well, you'll help keep a roof over your head," Grandma said.

"Unless the city comes along and takes the roof to make a park. Can sewing stop that?"

"Always roll the dough away from yourself, but you can't roll it more than three times."

"Grandma, did you hear what I just said?"

Grandma wiped her hands on her apron. "Yes, I heard

you, and I read the article in the paper, too. It's the same old story."

Maria stopped peeling the apple and looked at her grandmother. "But, Grandma . . ."

"Listen, I read the papers, but I don't need to read papers to know that this thing is going to happen. Just as it happened when my people first came here."

Maria knew which story was coming next. Papa always said that Grandma was talking about events that had happened almost two hundred years ago, before Grandma's own grandmother was born.

"We were never slaves. We come from Angola and spoke Portuguese."

Maria kept peeling apples, and Grandma carefully set the dough in the baking pan as she continued telling her story.

"My people were indentured servants. They worked for the Dutch and owned all the land around here past the City Hall. Everyone called our area Land of the Blacks. Because all of them had their own farms. Then the British came, passed a law that Africans can't own land, and that's the end of the Land of the Blacks." She stared at Maria and leaned toward her as if to make her understand every word. "You may as well face the truth. The city will do what it wants. Some of us moved uptown, but the city built a reservoir, so they had to leave there, too."

Maria always liked the way Grandma would tap her forehead when she was ending her story and say, "I keep the memory."

Maria carefully rolled the apples in the piecrust and kept reminding herself that Grandma could have been mistaken. "Tell me again how you named us," she said.

"I named your mother Catalina, after my own mother. And I named some of you children after the ancestors. I named Moosa after your grandfather. He was a pure African, and that's the African way to say Moses. And you, Maria. I named you, too, after my old aunt."

"Why?" Maria asked knowing the answer, but always wanting Grandma to repeat it.

"Because you are a tall, beautiful tree, as she was. I named Diana after a cousin. Now, Elizabeth and Simon, your papa gave them those British names."

Maria sighed, and Grandma cupped her long face in her hands. "Don't worry, my dear. At least the city will pay your papa for his property. We were never paid for ours. Your papa will have enough money to find you a new home, perhaps a better home somewhere."

Maria only wanted the home she had.

CHAPTER 4

COLORED SCHOOL
NUMBER THREE

O N MONDAY MORNING, Maria, Elizabeth, and Diana walked down Cedar Lane, huddled together for warmth. They waved at the other children coming out of the small frame houses that sat along the rutted dirt road. Their neighbor, Byron, dashed down his porch steps.

"Hi!" he shouted as he ran down the lane. "Let's have a snowball fight this afternoon, Maria!"

"I'll pummel you good!" she shouted back.

"Yeah! My sister will get you!" Diana giggled, and she ran ahead to walk with some of the little girls in her grade. They passed Amelia Davis's large, three-story house. Maria didn't see Amelia, the Monitor General, who usually went to school early to help Miss James.

Elizabeth pulled on her arm. "Why do you like to

throw snowballs with the boys like that?"

"It's fun."

"Miss James said . . ."

"Oh, Miss James is too fussy, Lizzie. We'll just go behind the school where she won't see us."

They walked carefully down the hill. The rocks, crags, and broken-down shanties in the distance were covered with a white quilt of snow. The clear blue sky, the patches of green pine needles, and the cedar grove next to the Magpie's house provided the only color.

"Isn't this a pretty morning, Lizzie?" Maria asked.

"Yes. There's no dirt anywhere. Everything looks so clean."

But as soon as Maria entered the school yard, she began to dread the week. It was such a long way to Saturday—her birthday.

Diana stood near the front of the line, with the younger girls. When Miss James walked over to Mr. Clark, the headmaster, to speak to him, Diana showed the girls in her group the steps of the dance she'd seen on Sunday on the way to Grandma Isabella's house. She imitated the dance perfectly, picking up her skirt and quickly crossing her feet one over the other. The girls in her group laughed until Miss James came back. Then they quickly quieted down.

One day Diana is going to get into trouble with her foolishness, Maria thought, as she looked on, amused at Diana's antics.

Elizabeth, standing with a group of girls, had already removed the speller from her basket. They had been assigned to demonstrate a spelling and a grammar lesson for the examiners, so she had been allowed to bring the speller home for practice.

Maria stood behind her classmate, Sarah, in the back of the line, with the other older students. Maria and Sarah were among the few senior girls who were not monitors and not in the Class of Merit; Sarah's arithmetic was as bad as Maria's sewing.

The six monitors, all senior girls who helped the head-mistress, gathered their groups of pupils in preparation for entering the building. Each day it became more difficult for Maria to walk behind the monitors instead of leading her own group of girls into the school. And for some reason, today it seemed to bother her more than ever.

Sarah turned around. "Hi, Maria. Have you heard that the city is going to tear down our homes and everything around here?" Her eyes grew large as they always did when she was excited.

"It was in the paper, but my papa said it was just a rumor." Maria tried to sound calm and confident.

"My father said the same thing." Sarah's eyes grew even wider. "I wonder what happened to the other girls in our form?"

Maria shrugged. "I don't know. They're absent a lot. Maybe they had to mind their sisters and brothers or go to work."

They started to walk in. Sarah kept talking. "Well I like it when it's just you and me," she said. "Then Miss James can see how silly it is to keep us from being monitors just because I can't cipher and you can't sew."

Maria nodded. "We'll be a class of two and monitor each other. I'll do your math, and you will do my sewing."

They entered the passageway. Wood, for the stoves that warmed each of the two rooms in the building, was stacked in a corner. A table and bench sat on either side of the passageway, for those times when students received special tutoring or when one of the monitors needed a place to prepare the students' lessons.

There were two rooms off the passageway—the large room where classes and programs were held for the eighty-five girls in the school, and a smaller room where the headmistress conducted special lessons for the monitors, and met with visitors, parents, and students who misbehaved.

Miss James stood with her arms folded and her face unsmiling as she watched the girls file in, with the monitors leading. They walked straight to the large closets in the back of the room. Amelia Davis stood behind Miss James.

The girls hung their cloaks on pegs and took their seats.

Maria glanced at Diana. Her face was serious, the laughter gone. After being made to stand in a corner with her back to the class a few times, she'd learned not to play once she set foot in the classroom. Elizabeth always behaved perfectly.

Once the girls were settled in their seats with their notebooks in front of them, Miss James picked up the

Bible from her desk. In her smooth, melodious voice, so different from her stern appearance, she said, "Girls, today's Bible reading is from Psalm thirty-four, verses one through four." Everyone listened silently as she read. When she finished the Bible reading, she looked even more serious than usual. She held her head high, and her back was as straight as a board. She was so light-skinned she looked like a white woman.

"Class, we have a new student in our school: Anna Holmes. Anna, dear, stand before the class and say hello." Anna mumbled hello to the class, who returned her greeting; then she returned to her seat.

Maria was surprised to see the same girl who had been in church on Sunday, and was reminded of Sojourner Truth. The thing that Maria hadn't noticed on Sunday was that the girl was tall, like herself. She was very thin and wore boots so old that they turned to the side. She had on the same rumpled dress and blue shawl she had worn on Sunday. Maria wondered whether she had worn a cloak to school. She hadn't noticed her going to the closet, or even in the lineup outside the building.

Maria whispered to Sarah, who sat next to her, "Did she line up with us this morning?"

"No. You couldn't have missed her," Sarah whispered back.

Anna looked about thirteen or fourteen years old, yet she sat with the young ABC pupils. Maria put herself in the girl's place and understood how ashamed she must have felt, towering over the little ones and shabby from head to foot. Maria understood why she hadn't noticed her before.

There was something sad about the way her thin shoulders slumped. She looked so strange and awkward sitting there with the younger children, who stared at her.

Sarah nudged Maria. "She's the oldest ABC student I've ever seen," she said, with a giggle in her voice.

"You shouldn't laugh at her, Sarah."

"I'm not really laughing at her. I wonder which monitor Miss James will ask to help her?" Sarah asked.

Miss James sharply shushed everyone, but Sarah whispered to Maria again. "Everyone is trying to finish their projects for the exams. No one has time to help her, and there are no extra monitors."

"Girls, take out your compositions," Miss James ordered.

As Maria watched the writing monitor collect the composition papers, she sat up very straight and raised her hand as high as she could. "Miss James," she called out, "may I speak with you?"

Miss James frowned as she took the papers from the monitor. "What is the matter? Can it wait?"

"No, Miss James. This is very important."

"Come down here."

Maria walked down the aisle, holding her head high, just as Miss James did. She was taller than Miss James and didn't mind looming over her when she wanted something. Maria lowered her voice so the other girls wouldn't hear. "Miss James, can I help the new girl with her ABCs?"

CHAPTER 5

THE NEW GIRL

A T FIRST, MISS JAMES looked at her as if she hadn't heard correctly. "Is this what you call important, Maria?"

"Well, yes, Miss James. I know how busy all the monitors are because of the exams, and I thought I could help."

"Aren't you busy, too, Maria?"

"I've completed all of my work."

Miss James folded her arms and stared at Maria for a moment. "What about your shirt?"

"I'm finished, Miss James."

"I think this is just a way for you to feel like a monitor. The only reason you're not a monitor is your poor sewing skills."

Maria sighed and lowered her head so that Miss James couldn't read her thoughts. *It's called plain sewing, so why must I have perfect stitches, anyway?* "Miss James, I finished my shirt. Can I please help the new girl?"

Miss James glanced at Anna, who sat with her hands folded and her head down. The monitors were with their students, reviewing spelling exercises. "I'll let you help her for a while this morning, and I'll check your sewing later."

Maria wanted to leap around the classroom.

Miss James handed Maria a slate, a ruler, and a piece of chalk. "There's nothing I'd like better than to make you a monitor, but you must improve your sewing!"

She turned to the new girl. "Anna, this is your classmate, Maria, and she's going to show you the alphabet."

Anna kept her head bowed, "Yes, ma'am," she said softly.

Miss James stared at the top of Anna's bowed head for a moment and then lifted her chin. "You must look a person in the eye when he or she talks to you, and we don't say *ma'am* here. It's 'Yes, Miss James.'"

"Yes, ma'am, Miz James."

Maria wondered at the strange way the new girl talked. *Ma'am* certainly seemed okay to her. She liked the sound of it.

"Maria, you remember how we teach the alphabet lessons."

"Yes, Miss James. I remember perfectly. I'm teaching my little brother at home."

"You and Anna can work at the table in the hallway."

Maria felt all eyes on them as they walked up the aisle and out into the passageway to begin Anna's very first lesson. *What wonderful luck*, Maria thought, believing that this was the first step toward becoming a monitor in spite of what Miss James said about her sewing.

She drew lines on the slate as she had seen Miss James and the monitors do for the little ones and as she remembered having learned herself. Anna watched intently as Maria drew her perfectly straight lines. She spoke as she drew the lines. "Anna, you've never learned how to read and write?"

"I never been to school."

"Oh," Maria said. Her mother's words rang in her head: *A lot of the colored children in this city never go to school, because they have to work. Those white children, too, going through Eighty-fifth Street and all about here picking rags and selling newspapers, can't go to school, either.*

Maria finished drawing the lines on the slate, and almost sounding like Miss James, she said, "there are twenty-six letters in the alphabet, and the letters stand for the sounds we make when we speak."

Anna nodded. "Yes, ma— . . . uh . . . Maria."

Maria smiled at her. "You were going to say, 'ma'am,' weren't you?"

"It's what my mother trained me to say, especially to my elders."

Maria put down the chalk. "I'm not your elder. I bet we're the same age."

"Yes. I think so, but you're showing me things I don't know."

"I'm twelve and will be thirteen on Saturday," Maria said proudly. "How old are you?"

"I'm thirteen, too."

"Where are you from?"

"New York," Anna replied quickly. "We moved here from Baxter Street."

"My grandmother lives downtown, on Leonard Street. Baxter Street is around the corner."

"Yes. I know where Leonard Street is," Anna said, looking away from Maria.

"Are you related to Miss Truth, who spoke in church on Sunday?"

"Oh, no. I never seen her before." She glanced at the slate. "Maybe you better show me the writing now."

Maria thought about all of the poor children she'd seen every time they went to Grandma Isabella's. Was Anna among them? She couldn't ask her that. She was sure she would hurt her feelings if she did. But she had a feeling that downtown was not the only place that Anna was from.

"Where do you live now?"

"A little way down the hill from here."

"Oh," was all Maria said, realizing that Anna probably lived among the swampy grounds and shanties they had traveled through when they were going down the hill to Seventy-ninth Street.

"I like the sound of the word *ma'am*," Maria said. "Sounds like a bleating lamb, almost. We'll call each other ma'am, since you like saying it. And I don't see anything wrong with you saying it."

Anna smiled, showing deep dimples in her chin.

Her wide smile with her straight, flawless white teeth made her face look pretty in its own way.

"The first letter is *A*." Maria wrote a large capital *A*. She had impeccable handwriting and showed Anna how to form the letter. "You write it like this, Anna. Begin here. One line going down, and then another line going this way. And then a small straight line between the longer ones. Your name, Anna, has two letter *A*'s in it. You didn't know that, did you?"

"No, ma'am." Anna chuckled.

"Well, ma'am," Maria said, "I'll show you later how to write your name, but for this morning, we'll practice the letter *A*."

"Yes, ma'am," Anna said, and both girls giggled.

Maria noticed how large Anna's hands were. They had old and new scars, and looked almost like a man's hands, not a young girl's. Maria placed Anna's fingers on the piece of chalk, showing her how to hold it between her thumb, index, and middle fingers. She guided her hand over the slate, showing her how to form the lines for the letter *A*.

Maria's morning was not so long or miserable after all. Amelia brought Maria her work—a new composition for the following day and some new arithmetic problems.

"Miss James said to give these to you," she said, handing Maria the homework.

Amelia held her back straight and her head high, just like Miss James, as she walked away.

"Is she a teacher, too?" Anna asked.

"No, but she thinks she is. She's the head monitor and

tries to act like Miss James. We call her Little Miss James, or Little Miss, for short."

"And she is short as a tree stump," Anna chuckled.

Maria threw her head back as her laughter filled the hallway, just as Miss James came to check on them.

"Are you girls playing or working?"

"We're working, Miss James," Maria said, holding the slate up for Miss James to see. The teacher's face almost softened into a smile when she saw what Anna had written so far. Her *A*'s were barely legible until the last line. Slowly, the letter began to emerge. "This is good, dear. You've never held a piece of chalk or a quill, have you?"

"No, ma'am, I mean, Miz James. Never have."

Miss James nodded approvingly at Maria. "You're teaching her well."

"Miss James, can I help Anna this afternoon?"

"Yes, but I'll be checking your sewing."

The church bells rang twelve times. "It's time to get our dinner baskets, Anna, so we can have lunch and then go outside."

"Dinner basket?"

"Yes. Didn't you bring your lunch?"

Anna shook her head and lowered her eyes again. "No," she mumbled, holding her head down. "I'm not hungry. I'll wait here till you come back, ma'am." She gave Maria a weak smile.

"You're not hungry?"

She shook her head. "I'll practice the writing."

When Maria went back into the classroom, Sarah and Amelia and several other girls pounced on her with questions.

"What is the new girl like? How old is she?"

"She's nice and she's the same age we are."

"She looks so strange. Where is she from?"

"Downtown," Maria said, taking her dinner basket out of the closet.

"She looks like she's from farther away than that," Amelia said, sliding into her seat and opening her basket.

Maria thought so, too, but she didn't like agreeing with Little Miss, who thought she knew everything. She sat down with Little Miss, Sarah, and Naomi, the arithmetic monitor, and Naomi's younger sister, Emily, who was Elizabeth's best friend. When they ate inside, the girls would sit wherever they wanted to in the room. Sometimes, younger girls would go to the back of the room and sit with their older sisters. Diana had her own little friends and ate with them in the front of the room.

"Does Anna live on Cedar Lane?" Elizabeth asked.

"Of course not," Maria said. "We would've seen her."

All of the girls had made their own dinner baskets, and each one was fancier than the next. Some were made of beads, moss, straw, and even cardboard, bound with shiny gilt paper and decorated with ribbons and dried flowers. Maria owned one of the prettiest baskets. Elizabeth had made it for her and woven pink and yellow ribbons into the straw and pasted colorful beads onto the ribbons.

The room was filled with laughter and talk and looked

like an indoor picnic, despite the eight large lesson charts hanging from the ceiling in front and the two blackboards on stands on either side of Miss James's desk.

Sarah turned to Maria. "So, what do you want to play when we go outside?"

Maria thought for a moment. "I want to have a snowball fight with the boys. The girls against the boys."

Naomi wiped her mouth. "They put ice in the snowballs, and they throw too hard."

Maria took a bite of cheese and brown bread and talked with her mouth full the way her mother always told her not to do. "You're too prissy. That's why they always bother you." Suddenly she thought about Anna sitting in the hallway alone with no lunch. She stood up.

"Where are you going?" Elizabeth asked.

"Come outside to the hall, Lizzie. You, too, Sarah. Let's eat lunch with the new girl out there."

Sarah took a bite of her apple. "I don't feel like moving now. I'm going outside when I'm done. But no snowball fight for me."

Little Miss stared at Sarah. "You don't want to have a snowball fight with that tall beanpole boy you like?"

They all laughed. "I'll come to the yard after I eat," Maria said. Elizabeth followed her.

Miss James entered the room as they were leaving. "Where's Anna?" she asked.

"In the hall," Maria said. "We're sharing our lunch with her. She doesn't have any."

Miss James seemed to be a little disturbed, but didn't

say anything, except, "That's nice of you both. A little kindness goes a long way. Today, I'll let you eat out there. But Anna has to accustom herself to all of the students."

Anna was still writing when Maria and Elizabeth walked over to her. Maria put her basket on the table and stood over her with her arms folded. "Anna, this is my sister Lizzie. We're going to share our lunch with you."

"But I had a big breakfast this morning."

"I insist, ma'am. If you don't eat with us, we'll be very insulted."

Anna relented, and Maria and Elizabeth shared their cheese and brown bread with her. Both sisters tried to give her an apple, but she wouldn't take anything else from them.

Miss James emerged from her office and came over to them. She handed Anna a slice of cake for dessert. Anna looked as though she might cry. "Thank you so much, ma'am. Thank you."

"Tomorrow, dear, I want you to eat inside the classroom. Meet some of the other students," Miss James said, and she left.

Maria could hear the girls' voices and knew they were playing I Spy. She heard them yelling, "Whoop," and then a lot of squealing and laughing. She could also hear the bat against the ball as the boys played baseball. "What kind of games do you play, ma'am?" she asked Anna.

"Never play games."

Maria and Elizabeth looked at each other with questioning glances.

"You never played Wash My Lady's Dresses, or Jacob, Where Are You? Or blindman's buff or Hunt the Squirrel, or Here I Bake and Here I Brew, or I Spy?" Maria rattled off the names of their favorite games.

Anna's eyes brightened for a moment. "Some of the children on the farm where I lived play I Spy, but I never did."

"Farm? I thought you lived downtown before you came up here," Maria said.

"Well, I . . . I . . . I . . . lived on a farm when I was very little. I don't remember exactly where it was," Anna said.

Elizabeth said, "Well it's too cold to go outside anyway, so I'll read us a story until classes start." She went to the small library in Miss James's office.

"Anna, you never played tag a little bit? For a minute?" That was Maria's favorite game, because she could outrun everyone, even the boys.

Anna shook her head.

Elizabeth came back with a book, *Tanglewood Tales for Girls and Boys*. While Maria liked the fanciful stories about Greek gods and heroes, she'd rather have been outside; for some reason, though, she felt responsible for Anna and sat in the passageway, listening to Elizabeth read and watching Anna trying to perfect the letter *A*.

When Elizabeth stopped reading to take a breath, Anna said, "I can tell us a story." The passageway seemed to get completely quiet, and the sounds of the children playing outside and those in the classroom seemed to disappear as Anna began her story, straight from her head.

❄ CHAPTER 6 ❄

ANNA'S STORY

ONCE UPON A TIME *there was an old man who lived deep in the piney woods in a log cabin by hisself. He'd been hunting all day, but didn't catch a thing—not even a squirrel. He was hungry as could be. All he had was some greens, didn't even have a piece of fat meat to flavor them. So while he setting there watching that pot of greens boiling, he hears a rustlin' behind him. He turns around quick and sees the strangest-looking critter sliding between the cracks in the logs of the cabin. This strange critter, though, had a big, furry tail. The old man picked up his ax and whacked off the critter's tail as it slithered out of the cabin.*

The man throw that tail in the pot of greens,

*and when the tail cook up good, the man eat him
a bellyful. It was sure enough good. The man was
so full he start to fall asleep. But when the sleep
was getting deep, suddenly the man was jolted
awake. He hear something wailing and crying
in the wind. It was like the wind was screaming,
"Tailypo, tailypo. Give me back my tailypo." Then
it sound like the wailing is in the cabin. "Give me
back my tailypo."*

Elizabeth and Maria both jumped at the same time.
Anna's high-pitched wail truly sounded like some strange
thing crying in the wind.

*The man got scared and flung open the cabin
door and let his dogs in. The dogs chased the
thing down to the swamp, and the man fell back
asleep. But then he hear a rattlin' and a rustlin'.
The wind start wailing again, "Tailypo, tailypo,
give me back my tailypo." The man sit up in his
bed and call his dogs, but they don't come. "Foolin'
around in that swamp," he tell hisself and went
back to sleep.*

*Then the man hear a gnawing sound on his
bed and a gnashing of teeth. Seem like something
is whooshing over his head and crawling up his
bed. He open one eye, too scared to open both, and
he see this critter with long, long, pointy ears, and
a big snout, beady red eyes, the smallest sharpest*

teeth you ever did see, and a stump where the tail used to be.

Maria and Elizabeth shuddered, but leaned toward Anna so that they wouldn't miss a word.

Then the critter jumps on the man's pillow and gets up right closer than we is, Maria and 'Lizabeth, and the critter say, "Tailypo, tailypo, give me back my tailypo."

And the man can't hardly speak between his chattering teeth. Finally he say, "I, I, I, ain't, ain't, ain't got no tailypo."

"You got it. You know you got it, and I wants it back," the critter growled at the man.

Now this critter had no sense when it got angry. "Give it back," it hissed, and it growled again.

"I . . . I . . . I don't, don't . . ."

The critter didn't even let the man get his words out. It tore up the man and it tore up that cabin. And on windy nights down in the piney woods, if you listen closely, you can hear a cry in the wind. "Tailypo, tailypo, I got me back my tailypo."

Maria clapped her hands as if she'd just seen a good play, and Elizabeth put her hand to her heart. "Oh, my, Anna. That was a scary story."

Then Maria, imitating Anna's wail, cried, "Tailypo, tailypo, bring me back my tailypo!"

For the first time that day, Anna laughed—a real laugh. Maria and Elizabeth joined her, and all three girls repeated, "Tailypo, tailypo, give me back my tailypo." Maria wondered how a girl who did not even read her own name could recite such a wonderful story.

The church bells rang twice. Lunch was over. This was the first time that Maria had ever stayed in through the whole lunch recess when she didn't feel like bursting through the walls. Elizabeth returned to the classroom, but Maria remained with Anna. "Well, ma'am, the *A* looks better, so now I'll show you the next letter."

She took the chalk out of Anna's hand. "The next letter is *B*. And it goes this way." Maria made a perfect letter *B*. She was pleased with herself as she greeted her schoolmates coming back from lunch. But just as she'd settled down next to Anna, taking her hand and showing her how to write the letter *B*, Sarah came dashing toward them from the classroom. "Maria, Miss James wants to see you. She's inspecting our sewing."

Maria wasn't worried. Her shirt was finished, and since she was helping Anna, she was sure Miss James would not give her another sewing project so close to examinations. She went back to the classroom and took out her sewing basket. The girls' sewing baskets were even larger and fancier than their dinner baskets. One girl had a basket made of feathers. Elizabeth had helped Maria make and decorate her basket with some small shells Papa had given them.

Maria sat in her seat impatiently, waiting for Miss James to call on her. Finally, the teacher called her to her desk. Maria tried to read her face. She looked for a smile, but found only a scowl.

"Now, Maria, you will never get anywhere in life as a woman if you do not learn how to sew." She held up the garment. "This is a haphazard shirt, if I ever saw one." Someone snickered, and Miss James glared at the girls. "Unless the rest of you girls have flawless garments, you have no business laughing. Maria, I want you to take the stitches out and redo the entire shirt. This is part of your examination."

Maria felt like hanging her head the way Anna did. "Miss James, I just started showing Anna how to write the letter *B*. She can write *A* backwards and forwards, Miss James."

"You can teach her and still do your sewing."

Maria walked back into the hallway. She sat down beside Anna and showed her how to form the letter *B*. While Anna practiced, Maria took out her haphazard shirt.

"What are you doing, ma'am?" Anna asked as she held the chalk over the slate.

"My sewing. I have to take the shirt apart, because Miss James doesn't like it." She sighed. "I wish I could just make it disappear."

Maria didn't notice the little gleam in Anna's eyes. "Maybe we give it to the tailypo."

Anna giggled, but Maria wasn't in a laughing mood.

Then Maria said, "Tailypo, tailypo, come on and eat this shirt."

Anna stopped writing for a moment and watched Maria's expression change into a frown, as she pulled the stitches out of her shirt. "I take the stitches out for you."

"I can't let you do my work."

"But you help me. Why can't I help you?"

"It's against the rules. We have to do our own sewing."

"So, if your shirt is sewed wrong, you get a paddling?"

"A paddling?"

"Yes. A whipping."

"No. We don't get whipped. Not in school. We just won't be promoted to the next sewing class."

"Is that bad?"

"Yes. My mama and papa would be angry with me."

"Well, give me your basket to take home, and I take the stitches out for you. Then you just have to sew tomorrow."

"We're supposed to leave our sewing in school until after examinations," Maria said. But she knew that some of the girls snuck their sewing home anyway—hiding it in their dinner baskets. All Anna was offering to do was to take out stitches. She wasn't doing the sewing. *What was so bad about that?* she asked herself.

The church bells struck five times. Maria watched as Anna walked down the hill toward a cluster of broken-down shanties that looked as if they might collapse in the slightest breeze. Anna, clutching her shawl tightly to her, turned around and waved at Maria and Elizabeth.

"She still doesn't have a cloak," Maria said.

"Maria, what is that bulge under her shawl? I thought she didn't have a basket," Elizabeth asked. Anna disappeared behind an outcropping of rock.

Maria spotted Diana racing up the hill toward Cedar Lane with her friend Amy and their other classmates. "She has my sewing basket. But don't tell Diana; you know she can't keep her tongue still. Anna is going to take out the stitches in my shirt for me."

"Miss James won't like that."

"Anna and I are helping one another. She's just removing the stitches. You know how slow I am. This way, I'll have the rest of the week to finish the shirt."

"Suppose she's absent tomorrow?"

That was the one thing that annoyed Maria about her sister. She always thought of the worst thing that could happen. "She'll be there. I'm sure of it. If she's absent, well, then I'll say the tailypo ate it."

"You'll be in trouble."

"I'm not going to think about the worst that could happen. I'm going to think about the best." It began to snow lightly, dusting the bare tree branches, and the evening shadows were darkening the sky. A couple of horses and wagons rattled up the hill. Maria watched to see whether it was Papa or Moosa, coming home early. But it was neither. The girls passed Little Miss's large house, and Byron passed them. "What happened today? I thought we were going to have a snowball fight. You're afraid to come out?"

"Byron, I am not afraid of you. I'll get you tomorrow," Maria grinned. She and Elizabeth trudged ahead, while Diana ran along with her friends. "If Anna doesn't show up then I'll have to tell Miss James the truth, Lizzie."

But deep in her heart of hearts she was sure that Anna would be there.

⊰ CHAPTER 7 ⊱

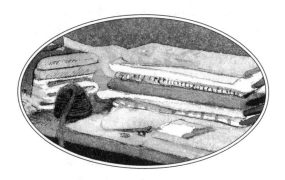

MAMA'S STORE

A S THE GIRLS WALKED along the road to their house, Byron threw a mushy snowball in their direction. Maria and Elizabeth ignored him. Simon, bundled up in his scarf, hat, and gloves, ran out of the yard to meet them. "Moosa is home, and Mama made some cider cakes." Dukie raced behind him, furiously wagging his tail.

Diana bent down and hugged Dukie. They all ran around to the back of the house to their mother's general store.

It was the family store, but Papa had always referred to it as "Mama's store," and the name stuck. Mama was the heart and soul of it, anyway.

Maria was the first one inside. "Moosa!" she shouted. "Why are you home so early?"

He sat on the bench drinking a cup of tea and eating a slice of cider cake. Mama was near the counter that ran from one wall to the other, hanging up a secondhand jacket and several plain dresses that Moosa had traded for the socks and mittens she and the girls had made.

"Hello, my sweets," she said stepping behind the counter.

"I'm not home to stay," Moosa said. "I finished trading in the stores downtown. I'm going to Farmer Gruner's to help him pack potatoes for tomorrow."

Suddenly, the store was filled with activity. The children hung up their outer clothing on pegs near the door, and Maria began to pour the tea. Mama placed slices of cider cake on the table in front of the bench where Moosa sat. He and Papa had built the bench and table in a corner of the room near the potbellied stove. They had also put up the yellow wallpaper, which made it seem as if the sun was always shining in the store.

Mama's store was small, serving the families who lived near Cedar Lane. The housewives especially liked to go to Catalina's, as they sometimes called the store, when they ran out of threads, needles, pins, buttons, scissors, and pieces of lace—or when they needed one or two eggs, a few slices of cheese or a cup of buttermilk, or just a smile and some friendly conversation.

Mama had a few books that Papa had picked up from the various secondhand stores.

Moosa glanced at the bookshelf behind the counter. He picked up a volume and read the long title out loud: *"The Gold Seeker's Manual, a Practical and Instructive Guide to*

All Persons Emigrating to the Gold Diggings in California."

Maria sipped her tea. "Maybe it will tell you how to find gold out west," she said.

Diana looked up at Moosa. "You're going to find gold?"

Mama smiled at her son. "When your father bought the book home yesterday, I knew you'd want it."

"Did he bring it for me?" Moosa asked, skimming through the pages.

"Now, Moosa, I don't think he paid much mind to the title. The book is in good condition; that's all he was thinking about. You know how he feels about that looking-for-gold business."

Mama straightened out the bolts of plain linen and woolen material. Sweaters, caps, socks, mittens and scarves that she and the girls had knitted were displayed on the counter. Jars of cinnamon, nutmeg, cloves, dried lemon peel, marjoram, parsley, garlic, and pepper were lined up on shelves behind the counter.

Maria only half listened to their conversation. This was one of her favorite times of the day. She liked sitting there in the soft yellow light of the kerosene lamp, eating the tasty cake and growing warm from the hot tea.

When she finished, she walked over to the clothing rack. She hoped her mother had a cloak that she could give Anna. Mama didn't believe in store-bought clothes, so she didn't have much clothing to sell. She'd give the secondhand clothing Papa brought home to some of the poorer families around them. "I think it's more important to sell sewing supplies, so that the ladies can make clothing for their families," she always said.

"Maria." Her mother's voice interrupted her thoughts. "How was school today?"

"There's a new girl, and Miss James is letting me teach her the alphabet."

"Maria, that's good. I told you Miss James would make you a monitor, if you just tried."

"I'm just helping her for now. I'm not really a monitor."

"Not yet, but you'll be one. You're going in a good direction."

Elizabeth rested her cup on the table. "This new girl told us a good story. Tell them, Maria. You're better at telling stories than I am."

Maria finished her tea and stood in the middle of the store. "Simon, Diana, listen to this." She told the tailypo story.

Diana's little mouth opened in surprise when Maria finished.

Moosa clapped. "That was good, Maria. Real good."

Mama shivered. "What a disgusting story."

But Diana twirled around and contorted her pretty face as if she were angry, and in an eerie, high-pitched voice, wailed, "Tailypo, tailypo, give me back my tailypo." Simon imitated her, singing out the refrain, and everyone except Mama laughed.

"Oh what foolishness," she said. "Tell a better story than that one, Maria."

They were still chuckling and Diana was chanting, "Give me back my tailypo," when the bells that Moosa had hung on the inside of the door tinkled, and one of Mama's regular customers, Byron Francis's mother, walked in. "Good evening, everyone. Catalina, I need half a dozen eggs."

Simon finished eating and pulled Maria's sleeve. "Tell the story again," he demanded.

"It's time for your lessons," Maria reminded him, opening his reader.

Elizabeth gathered the cups. Diana scooted behind the counter and stood next to Mama. She started folding handkerchiefs that were already folded and straightening the combs and mirrors in a drawer that was already neat.

"Excuse me, Mrs. Francis," Mama said, and then turned to Diana. "Come now, Diana. You have to help Lizzie."

"Don't you need help, Mama?"

"Yes. Get six eggs out of the cellar for Mrs. Francis; then help Lizzie prepare supper."

Diana pouted, but she went down to the cellar to get the eggs, and Elizabeth went into the house. Moosa stood up, and Maria whispered to him, "Don't forget to remind Papa about the trip downtown on Saturday. Okay?"

He nodded and patted her hand. "Don't worry, I'll remind him."

Moosa left the store, and Mrs. Francis and Mama continued talking. Maria wished Mrs. Francis would hurry up and leave. This would have been a good time to talk to Mama about going to the meeting on Saturday. She listened to Simon read.

"You're reading so good. When Mrs. Francis leaves, I'll let you read to Mama," she said, hoping that no one else walked in.

Diana returned with the eggs, and Mrs. Francis left.

Maria said to her mother, "Mama, listen to how good Simon can read. Stand up, Simon. That's the way you'll have to read when you start school next year."

He stood proudly, clutching the reader. *"The sun is up,"* he read. *"The man has fed the bla—bla—black hen and the fat duck. Now the duck will swim in the pond. The hen has run to her nest. Let us not stop at the pond now, for it is hot. See how still it is! We will go to see Tom and his top."*

Mama stepped from behind the counter and hugged him. "My sweet baby can read."

He frowned. "Mama, I'm not a baby anymore."

She rubbed his head. "You'll always be my baby."

"Mama, can I go inside now? I want to read to Diana and Lizzie."

She smiled at him. "Okay, my sweet."

"Mama, I'll help you close," Maria said. "The jars need refilling."

"Yes, I don't think anyone else is coming to the store now. We'll have everything ready for tomorrow."

Maria walked to the back of the store where Mama kept the barrels of salted fish and beef and the sacks of spices. She refilled the pepper and cinnamon jars and rehearsed the way she'd ask her mother again about going downtown on Saturday.

As Maria walked to the front of the store and stepped

behind the counter, the bells tinkled. Mrs. Hamilton, the Magpie, rushed into the store. In her excitement, every-thing seemed to be standing on end—her hair, her bonnet, her coat and dress. She waved two envelopes.

"Catalina, they did it! They finally did it!" she screeched.

CHAPTER 8

THE LETTER

MARIA HAD SEEN the Magpie get excited before, but never like this. Mama took her gently by the arm and sat her on the bench. Mrs. Hamilton clutched her chest and handed Mama one of the envelopes.

"Mrs. Hamilton, what is the matter? Calm down," Mama patted her on her shoulder and sat down next to her.

The Magpie's bonnet had slipped to one side. Her words tumbled out of her mouth. "I went to the post office this afternoon to get the mail. I picked up mine, and the clerk gave me yours, and when I saw both were from the city I opened mine immediately." She clutched her chest again. "Oh, dear, we'll all be homeless in the street."

Maria gasped. Mama's hands shook as she tore open the letter.

"Mama, what does it say? Are we going to be homeless?" Maria stepped from behind the counter.

Mama didn't answer, but started reading the letter aloud.

> *Dear Sir:*
>
> *Property Owner of Lots numbers twenty-two and twenty-three in Block number 786 on Commissioners Map—lying between 85th and 86th Streets, Seventh and Eighth Avenues in the City of New York.*
>
> *The Mayor, Aldermen, and Commonalty of the City of New York, by virtue of an Act entitled "An Act Relative to Improvements in the City of New York," will be opening and laying out a public place between 59th and 106th Streets, and Fifth and Eighth Avenues in the City of New York. Your property is part of the area to be improved and developed. The Commissioners have assessed your property and deem that you will be awarded the sum of $2,335 for said property.*

Mama stopped reading here and stared straight ahead, stunned.

"Mama, what does this mean?"

Mrs. Hamilton answered for Mama. "It means that the thieves who run this city will be taking our property. That's what it means."

"It's just like the paper said, isn't it? Grandma was right."

The Magpie didn't give Mama a chance to answer. "I'm going to give them a fight. And I know Solomon will, too, Catalina. We're not squatters and immigrants like those Irish people down the hill."

Mama stood up. "Mrs. Hamilton, since we own our property, perhaps we can refuse," she said, her voice rising just a little. "I really thought that article was just a rumor."

Mrs. Hamilton stood up and straightened her hat. "You're right, Catalina. I'm going to the other neighbors. I guess everyone got their letter. I will fight this, if I have to go to City Hall myself."

The Magpie rushed out of the store, and Maria tried very hard not to laugh at her and cry at the same time. She swallowed the lump in her throat, determined to sound strong. "Mama, the city can't just make us leave, can they? Can they just throw us out of our house?"

Mama picked up the broom again and began to sweep furiously. "No. They're offering us money to buy the property."

Maria stood up, folded her arms, and thought about Grandma Isabella standing at the window. And she thought about Miss Truth. Walking. "Well, suppose Papa doesn't want to sell it. They can't force him, can they?"

"No. No. Of course not," Mama said, her voice rising higher as she created tiny swirls of dust on the floor.

"Mama, I don't want to move."

"I don't either, my sweet. But the important thing is, we are all together. You remember that."

Maria thought she heard her mother's voice crack as she grasped her mother's arm.

"I'll finish closing up for you, Mama, if you want to rest. Do you want me to make you some tea?"

"Oh, my sweet, thank you, but no rest for me. I'd better see how Lizzie and Diana are coming along." She walked to the back of the store, and then she walked back to Maria again. "My sweet, we won't say anything to the children just yet. They're not as understanding as you are. They'll be so upset." She smiled slightly. "After all, you'll be thirteen next week."

Mama rushed out of the store, and Maria put the broom in the corner. Alone now, she let the tears stream down her thin face as she watched the snow fall heavily. All the things she'd worried about were insignificant now—whether she could go to the meeting on Saturday, or whether Anna would show up with her sewing basket tomorrow; even the fact that she would soon be thirteen did not matter anymore.

When Papa and Moosa walked into the house about an hour later, Maria understood what her mother had meant when she'd said, "The important thing is, we are all together." She saw her mother hand Papa the letter. While they stood in the entryway by the door talking, Maria pulled Moosa aside and told him what had happened.

"Maria, this is not a terrible thing. I told you that before. We can move out west. Papa's getting money? How much?"

"I don't remember. It was a lot of money, but even so, I don't want to leave our home."

He put his arm around her. "Don't look so sad, sister. This is the best news."

She jerked away from him and crossed her arms. "How can you say that, Moosa? This is our home."

After they'd eaten supper, Papa called Maria, Elizabeth, and Moosa to the kitchen table. Simon and Diana played Rabbit on the Wall; they made shadow figures of a rabbit and a fox using their hands and the lamplight and quietly giggled as the fox tried to eat the rabbit. Elizabeth put down her knitting and whispered to Maria, "Did we do something wrong? What happened?"

"I think Papa just wants to tell us something," Maria said.

Her heart thumped hard in her chest as Papa looked at her, Moosa, and Elizabeth with tender eyes. "Since you are the oldest, your mother and I wanted to talk to you three first. Maria, I know you've already told Moosa, haven't you?"

"Yes, Papa," Maria said.

Elizabeth turned to Maria, "What happened? Why didn't you tell me, too?"

"Because I told her not to," Mama said. "I didn't want you to get upset."

The worry lines appeared on Elizabeth's forehead, and Papa took her hand in his. "Now, listen. We've received a letter from the city saying that they're going to build a park here. I know you'll hear a lot of talk when you go to school, so your mother and I wanted to tell you first."

Elizabeth still looked hurt. "But Maria knew."

Mama explained how that came to be, and Papa explained the rest.

"I don't want you to worry about any of this. I am going to talk to the other property owners in our area, and we're going to fight this. They cannot take the property from us and give us less than what it's worth."

"Suppose you got more money, Papa. What would you do then?" Maria asked.

"First, I'm going to talk to the neighbors. Perhaps if all of us sent letters to the city saying we do not want to sell our property, then the city would have to build a park somewhere else."

Moosa cleared his throat. "Papa, how much will the city pay you?"

Papa looked at the letter again. "Two thousand three hundred and thirty-five," he said.

Maria's eyes widened. "That's a lot of money isn't it?"

"This property is worth more," he said, "and it sounds like a lot, but, Moosa, I still have dreams of your going to college."

Moosa said nothing about Papa's dreams. Instead he said, "But, Papa, this is a wonderful thing that has happened. We could move west. You can get a lot more land than we'd ever get here in the city."

Maria almost laughed at the way Papa looked upward, as if he were begging God to give Moosa some sense. "Moosa, I don't know what's out west. I know what I have here, and I'm going to fight to keep it. Don't tell me anymore about the West."

"But, Papa, you remember when Frederick Douglass said that if one thousand free colored families settled in Kansas, the slaveholders would shun it, and the territory would stay free?" Moosa didn't wait for him to answer. "You remember you said it didn't sound like such a bad idea? I think it's a good idea, too, except there's no gold in Kansas."

Papa stood up, which was usually a sign that he was finished with explaining. "There's probably no gold anywhere. Only in those books you read. Kansas might be a good place for people who have no land or property. But we have property right here." He stared calmly at all of them. "Now, if we can't win a fight with the city, then I might consider Kansas."

For a moment Mama's large eyes flashed, and Maria knew that Mama wasn't necessarily interested in going to Kansas. But then she spoke softly, her voice neither high-pitched nor excited. "Whatever happens, we're together, and we will always take care of each other. And the important thing is not to worry about what will happen. Maria and Lizzie, I only want you to think about school right now."

Papa nodded. "Your mother is right. There's no need for you girls to worry, no matter what you hear at school tomorrow. And Moosa, my son, one day you'll be a doctor or lawyer. That's worth more than gold."

Moosa didn't answer.

The clock struck nine, and Mama reminded Simon

and Diana that it was time for bed. Elizabeth went upstairs as well.

Papa left the table and put his arm around Maria. "Maria, no more frowns and sad faces. Just think about that pair of socks you're making for me to sell."

With Papa's arms around her she felt better. "Can I go to the meeting with you and Moosa next Saturday? For my birthday?"

Mama heard her from the other side of the room; she and Papa asked at the same time, "Why?"

"I want to hear Miss Truth speak again. I'm not a baby anymore. Mama, you went when you were my age."

"And I was in the middle of a dangerous riot."

Papa's eyes were gentle as he smiled at Mama. "Well, this is 1855, not 1834. She'll be with me and Moosa. So if she does well with the examinations, she can come with us for her birthday."

"I'll be perfect," Maria promised.

By the time she settled down in the large bed she shared with her sisters, Maria had replaced her worries about losing their home with good thoughts about how wonderful it would be to go out with Moosa and Papa on Saturday. Maybe she'd see Miss Truth again. She was certain nothing would prevent her from going with them until she remembered the trouble she'd be in if Anna were absent from school tomorrow.

CHAPTER 9

AN UNEASY MORNING

ORTUNATELY, IT WAS not snowing the next morning when the girls left for school, but the ground was covered with a thin layer of ice. All three of them almost fell when they walked past the Magpie's boarding house. She was outside waving her hands excitedly as she talked to her next-door neighbor, Mrs. Francis.

Diana slipped, slid, and giggled as she made her way over to Amy, who was just stepping off her porch. Maria and Elizabeth walked down the road together, stepping carefully in icy spots. The closer they came to the paved pathway that led to the school, the more Maria began to think about what she'd say to Miss James if Anna were absent. "Lizzie, if Anna isn't there," she said, "perhaps I'll say that I picked up the wrong basket when we left yesterday afternoon, and I was in such a lather about it this morning I forgot it at home." She thought a moment. "I'll sneak my dinner basket into the closet."

"I don't think she'll believe you. You shouldn't tell lies like that." The cold made Elizabeth look as if she had rouge on her round, bronze cheeks.

"I know, Lizzie. It's just a little falsehood. I won't do it again."

"You're not supposed to lie. Mrs. Ball is always telling us that. Mama and Papa, too."

"But, Lizzie, if I tell the truth, Miss James will get so bothered. I don't want to upset her."

"You've just told another lie," Elizabeth said.

Maria immediately slid on an icy patch just beyond Little Miss's house. Elizabeth tried to catch her, and they both fell. Maria's dinner basket flew out of her arms, and her bread and some of the beads from the basket were strewn over the cold, wet ground. Elizabeth had managed to hold on to her basket.

Both of them tried to scramble to their feet quickly. Unfortunately, Byron and a group of boys slid by as though they were on ice skates. Byron saw them splayed out on the ground and laughed so hard he almost fell. The other boys joined in.

"Byron, if you don't get away from us I'll knock you into tomorrow," Maria shouted as she helped Elizabeth up.

Byron and the other boys kept laughing and shoving one another as they continued sliding down the path toward the school. Maria picked up her crushed basket, with some of the ribbons dangling and many of the beads missing, and kicked the ruined bread into a clump of bare twigs.

Elizabeth brushed off her cloak. "See what happens when you lie?"

"Byron is lucky it's so slippery out here. Otherwise, I'd chase him down the hill."

When they neared the school, it seemed as if everyone were racing and slipping on the ice and throwing snowballs. Only the senior girls and boys stood quietly talking among themselves. The children spun around the two buildings like little tornadoes instead of lining up. Maria searched for Anna among the crowd. It was hard to tell where she was, with everyone running and falling down on patches of ice.

"What is wrong with them?" Maria asked. "This is how they usually act after school, not before."

Diana walked ahead of them with Amy. Maria saw her and two other girls pretending to ice-skate on a large frozen puddle. She turned to Elizabeth. "Do you see Anna?"

"No. I don't see her anywhere," Elizabeth said, peering around.

"I guess I'll have to tell Miss James I took my basket home by mistake."

Suddenly, Elizabeth pulled Maria's sleeve. "Look, Maria. There she is."

Anna, wearing a cloak that was too big, stood near the senior girls. Maria was glad to see she had a cloak, and even more relieved to see that she was there.

Anna smiled and waved as she walked over to Maria. "I have your basket," she whispered.

Maria saw the bulge under Anna's large cloak. "Thank you, thank you, thank you!" She couldn't help grinning from ear to ear.

She glanced over at the boys lining up and saw Byron laughing and hopping around, then falling.

Sarah and several other girls in Maria's form rushed over to her. "Did your family get a letter?" Sarah asked, her eyes flashing. She didn't wait for an answer. "My father got one saying the city will tear down our houses. We don't know where we're going. Oh, what a terrible thing, Maria!"

Maria patted Sarah on the back. "Don't worry, Sarah. Our families will fight this. They won't let the city throw us out of our homes."

The students quieted down a little when Headmaster Clark and Miss James came and stood before them. Miss James shushed the girls as they all walked into the building. When they reached the classroom, Anna stepped into the closet before Maria did. When it was Maria's turn to hang up her cloak, she saw her sewing basket sitting there as if it had never been moved. She put her ruined dinner basket next to it and promised herself she'd never do such a thing again.

The room seemed unusually noisy for so early in the morning. The girls talked, and even the younger ABC pupils were fidgeting and moving around like little gnats. Maria stared at Diana, who was also yammering away.

Miss James clapped her hands. "Girls, girls. Please

settle down." She lowered her head as if she were praying, and the room grew quiet.

Miss James raised her head. "Girls, I think I know why you are so excited. It's about the city turning this area into a park."

Alice, a thin, quiet girl in the fourth form who was always coughing and sniffling, raised her hand. "Miss James, will they tear down our school?"

Emily's hand shot up. "Where will we go?" she asked.

"Girls, we do not know what will happen in the future. We can never know that, but we do know what we must do now. You children must prepare for your upcoming examinations. You may not be able to do anything about the city, but you can do something for yourselves. We have to think about today and the tasks before us, children. I want you girls to do well. So let's just focus on that for now."

Maria was surprised. Miss James wasn't usually so comforting.

The girls put their compositions on their desks, folded their hands, and lowered their heads as Miss James read from the Bible. Then, as happened every Tuesday morning, Miss James dictated spelling words to the senior girls, while the writing monitors did the same for the other groups. As the girls took dictation, Anna practiced writing the letters *A* and *B* on the slate Miss James had lent her. The girls grew quiet.

After dictation, the students read. Groups of five students from each of the eight reading forms stood around the lesson charts, as the reading monitors pointed to each word. When a student missed a word, another girl corrected her, taking a turn at reading until she made an error. The next girl corrected her and, if she read the entire lesson without a mistake, was promoted to a higher reading form.

Maria wasn't pulled out of her form, because she was already at the highest reading level and knew the lessons. She tried to ignore them and worked on her composition.

Naomi, the monitor of arithmetic, dictated addition and subtraction problems to the younger students. Anna recited the arithmetic with them. "One and one are two," Naomi said, holding up two fingers.

The students responded, "Two and one are three," holding up three fingers.

Then, Miss James dictated multiplication and division to Maria and the older girls.

Maria hoped that after their arithmetic exercises, she'd be able to help Anna again. Their next subject would be reading, and Maria was tops in reading. Surely, she thought, Miss James would let her help Anna for the rest of the morning. But she did not.

When the church bells chimed eleven times, Miss James stood before the whole school. "Girls, attention. For the rest of the morning and afternoon we'll rehearse for Friday's examination." Arms folded in front of her, Miss James gave her orders. "You girls who are doing the Bible reading and those of you doing the presentation from the English reader, go to the boys' building now."

These girls got up quickly, almost pushing one another out of the way as they rushed to the closet to get their cloaks. Maria and several other girls, remaining at their desks, practiced an arithmetic exercise for Examination Day. Naomi stood in front of Maria, Sarah, and three other girls in their form. "Girls, remember, no chalk or slate."

"We know," Maria said. She nudged Sarah. "You practiced at home, right?"

Diana was the last pupil to rehearse before lunch. She walked onto the platform, made a little twirl, and then curtsied. Miss James stopped her. "Now, Diana, just walk up to the stage, recite your poem, and only do one curtsy when you're finished. That's sufficient. You're not a ballerina."

By the time they finished practicing, it was twelve o'clock. "Maria, I think our group will do well, don't you?" Sarah asked.

"Yes. We're going to be the best," Maria said. Then, to herself, *If you don't forget how to multiply.*

As she walked to the closet, she heard Little Miss declare, "I made a new dress and apron, and I'm wearing them tomorrow."

The other girls laughed and talked about what they'd wear for Examination Day, as they headed to the closet for their dinner baskets. Maria's thoughts, though, were on her birthday outing with Moosa and Papa.

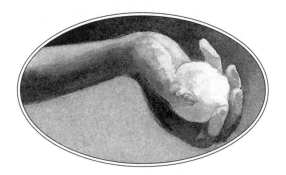

CHAPTER 10

THE FIGHT

MARIA TOOK HER dinner basket out of the closet and started to walk over to Sarah and a couple of the senior girls. But then she saw Anna sitting alone and walked toward her instead. "Where are you going?" Sarah asked.

"I'm going to eat with Anna."

Elizabeth followed Maria.

This time, Anna had some brown bread wrapped in a clean white cloth. "Have some cheese," Elizabeth said to her.

"I can't eat your lunch every day." Anna looked over at Maria. "Your basket is ruined. Where your bread?"

They told her what had happened.

Anna grinned slightly. "I fall, too. Some of them boys laugh at me." She broke a piece of bread and handed it to Maria. "Take some."

"Only if you take some of my cheese," Maria said. "Let's go outside after we eat. We'll get some of the girls and play I Spy, Anna."

"Maybe I just stay inside."

"No, ma'am. You have to come out and play."

Elizabeth stood up. "Maria, stop bossing. If Anna wants to stay in, leave her alone. I'm going outside, and if it's too cold I'll come back."

"The day will never end if we don't go outside," Maria said, turning to Anna.

"Ma'am," Anna said, "I want to know something. I hear the girls talking about everybody leaving. Your family leaving, too?"

Anna's question brought back all of the worrisome feelings that Maria had been trying to push aside. Maria tried to reassure herself and Anna at the same time. "Don't worry. My father and mother said the people will write the city letters and that the city can't take our property. Anyway, you are with your family. That's all that matters."

Anna was quiet, with a frightened, faraway look in her eyes that she quickly tried to hide from Maria's gaze. Maria understood, for she often did the same thing. Anna lowered her face. "My parents don't own where we live. But no one told them about moving. Will they tear down the school, too?"

"Maybe not. Maybe they'll leave our school and church. I guess you could still have a school and a church in a park," Maria said.

"I love it here more than any other place we ever

live," Anna said. "I don't want to move."

"I don't, either, so let's not talk about it. Let's not worry. As my parents said, as long as you are with your family, then you're home."

Anna looked pained.

"What's wrong?"

"Nothing," Anna said, lowering her eyes.

Maria felt that Anna was keeping something from her. She stood up. "Come on, ma'am. No more worrying. Let's go outside."

They took their cloaks out of the closet. Anna's looked so big and heavy, Maria didn't think she'd be able to run or play I Spy. She wouldn't even be able to hide.

When they stepped outside, everyone was romping and racing. The sun had warmed the school yard nicely, and the patches of ice and frozen puddles were gone. One group of boys had organized a ball game. Byron rushed over to Anna and Maria, pointing and chuckling, as soon as they walked out of the girls' building. He turned to several boys who were following him. "There she is!" he shouted, "the biggest, clumsiest girl in the world." The other boys laughed.

Maria felt the heat rising from her toes all the way to her head, but she tried to ignore the boys' taunts and turned to Anna. "See those girls over there? They're playing Wash My Lady's Dresses. Anna, it goes like this. You face me and . . ."

She felt a tap on her shoulder and turned around to face Byron.

"I just want to know one thing," he said loudly. "Was the ground hard or soft this morning?" Everyone roared with laughter again.

"I told you before, you'd better leave us alone, and don't ever touch me again." Maria put her hands on her hips.

Elizabeth tried to pull her away. "Maria. Don't get upset."

"You looked like a baby giraffe, laying down there." Byron pitched himself onto the ground, lying on his back with his legs and arms spread.

It seemed to Maria as if every tree, twig, boy, girl, and even stray dog were laughing in her face. Then Byron got up and tapped her on the shoulder again and ran across the school yard.

Maria knew she shouldn't, but she couldn't help herself: she lifted her cloak and dress and raced after him. Everyone else followed them, shouting and yelling. She thought she heard Elizabeth's voice in the distance, calling her, and she imagined that she heard her mother whispering in her ear, *That's not ladylike, Maria.* She flew behind him anyway.

She caught up to Byron, pounced on him, and knocked him to the ground just as she'd seen the boys do. Immediately, the other children crowded around, shouting as Maria held him down, beating him about the head and shoulders.

One large boy leaning over them said, "She's giving you a sound cuffing, son."

When Headmaster Clark strolled out of the boys'

building, everyone scattered throughout the school yard, away from the fighters. Anna pulled Maria off Byron. "You'd best stop now. The headman just walk out," she said.

Byron scrambled up off the ground and ran to join a crowd of boys racing toward Zion Church. Anna and Maria walked quickly behind the girls' building, with Elizabeth, Diana, and Sarah following.

Maria and Anna sat down on a large log under an oak tree. Diana laughed as she mimicked the way Maria had knocked Byron to the ground.

Elizabeth said, "You're lucky Headmaster Clark didn't see you two fighting."

Sarah kept repeating rapidly, "Are you okay, Maria? Are you okay?"

Anna grinned. "You should be asking Byron if he okay. Maria got the best of him."

All Maria could think about was that she was in trouble and wouldn't be able to go to the meeting with Moosa and Papa on Saturday. "I'm okay," she said.

Diana ran back to the front of the yard. Elizabeth sat down next to Maria.

"You're in trouble," she said.

Sarah shook her head. "Maybe not. Headmaster Clark didn't see you two fighting, and no one will tell Miss James." She started giggling. "Byron will leave you alone now."

Maria was on edge all afternoon, but neither Headmaster Clark nor Miss James said anything to her about the fight. The girls spent the rest of the afternoon practicing their presentations for Examination Day. One thing made Maria happy—there was no sewing. She was sorry, though, that she could not help Anna, because they were practicing.

When school ended, Maria, Elizabeth, and Anna left the building together.

Anna whispered to her. "The next time you have to fight that boy, I'll help you. And I know *A* and *B* perfect now." Then she waved good-bye and left the school yard. Maria was so surprised she didn't know what to say. She liked Anna now more than ever.

Diana walked over to them, her eyes sparkling with excitement. "You whipped Byron soundly."

"You'd better promise not to tell Mama and Papa," Maria warned her.

"If you're not mean to me. Otherwise I'll tell."

"I'm never mean to you."

"Yes, you are, sometimes."

"Just promise you won't say anything."

"Will you help me do my chores?" Diana looked at her slyly.

"That's blackmail," Maria said, gazing at an outcropping of rock. "Okay. I'll help you do your chores. But if you break your promise, I'll pounce on you just like I did Byron."

"I'm telling Mama and Papa you're threatening me."

Elizabeth frowned at her sister. "Don't be mean, Maria. Diana won't say anything." Instead of continuing to walk with them, Diana suddenly raced up the hill past the bare trees and bushes on either side of the lane.

For the second time that day, Maria felt the blood rushing from her head to her toes. She started to chase Diana, but Elizabeth stopped her. "She's not going to tell."

"She's my sister, but sometimes I want to wring her neck. I bet she's going to go straight to the store now and wag her tongue to Mama."

"No, she won't. There are too many things she'll try to get from you first," Elizabeth looked down at Maria's hem peeking out from under her cloak. "What are you going to tell Mama about your hem?"

"I'll have to say I fell down—that's not a complete lie, is it?"

"Well, maybe half a lie," Elizabeth said as they walked toward the houses lining either side of Cedar Lane.

CHAPTER 11

THE PETITION

MARIA'S HEART THUMPED fast and loud when she entered the store. Her mother was standing behind the counter folding a sweater, and Diana and Simon were taking off their cloaks and jackets. Mama looked up and said in her usual cheery voice, "Hello, girls. How was school today?"

"Good." Maria and Elizabeth answered at the same time. Diana kept eating her cupcake and said nothing. The little imp is keeping quiet, Maria said to herself. Otherwise her mother would have started fussing as soon as they entered the store.

"We had to rehearse for the examiners' visit," Elizabeth added.

Diana stood up, her mouth still full of cake. "I practiced my poem."

"Diana, finish eating first. You sound like a mush mouth," her mother laughed.

Maria relaxed a little, especially when Mama sent Diana to help Elizabeth prepare the supper. If Diana were going to say anything, she would've done so already. And if Headmaster Clark or Miss James were going to come to the house, they would've been there. The headmaster lived on the next road over from Cedar Lane.

As Maria gave Simon his reading lesson that evening, it seemed as though more people than usual strolled into the store, including Mrs. Hamilton.

Maria tried to concentrate only on Simon and his reading lesson. But as the various neighbors, mostly housewives, came in, she realized that they were doing more talking than buying. She caught only snatches of their words: "The city . . . our property . . . not enough money . . . a petition . . . a meeting . . ."

The Magpie's words, though, particularly captured Maria's attention. "Where will we go?" she cried out.

No one answered her.

Maria's nagging worries returned.

Still, by the time her mother had closed the store and Papa and Moosa came home, everything felt so normal and right that Maria relaxed. They were together after all. While Moosa read his new book on the West, she sat with Elizabeth and Diana, knitting the socks she'd promised her father. Maria took great pains to make the stitches even and tight. Just as the clock struck seven, Dukie barked, and there was a knock on the door.

As Papa stood up, Mama followed, motioning for Maria to come, too. "We're going to have a meeting with some of the neighbors, about our houses, my sweet." Her voice was high-pitched and her movements nervous. "You make some tea for our guests and tell Lizzie to keep Simon and Diana quiet."

"Yes, Mama," Maria said, "I'll help you. Then can I sit at the meeting, too?"

"Maria, fix the tea. I don't want you to worry your head about all of this."

Simon started to run toward the kitchen, but Maria stopped him. "You can't go in there now. Mama and Papa have company."

"Why?" Diana asked. "We never have company during the week."

Maria frowned. *Why is this girl such a pest?* "They're having tea. Why don't you and Simon play a game? Quietly."

Mama greeted everyone who came in, and Dukie sniffed them and then went back to his spot near the fireplace. Mr. Francis sat down at the table, and Maria wondered whether Byron had told his parents about their fight. *Mr. Francis might say something,* she thought. The Magpie and five other neighbors sat around the table. Even Farmer Gruner came.

It seemed strange to Maria to see him sitting there.

He'd never visited them before, only stepping into the entryway briefly to talk to Papa or Moosa. As Maria put wood in the stove, she heard Papa call her brother away from his book.

"Moosa, join us," he said.

Maria waited for him to call her, too. When he didn't, she wanted to demand that she be allowed to sit with them also. She imagined Grandma Isabella standing at the window, and Miss Truth walking, but even those images didn't give her much nerve.

As she poured water into the teakettle, she heard Mr. Francis say, "If we can get every property owner to sign a petition, maybe the city will build its park around us."

And then Papa added, "Besides taking our property, this city isn't paying us enough. This is highway robbery." His voice was unusually loud, startling Maria. Everyone seemed to agree with him.

Maria had trouble understanding Farmer Gruner's thick accent, but she understood when he said, "The city wants to pay me such a little money for mine eight acres."

The Magpie's voice was the most excitable of all. "This property my husband left me is all that I have in the world! This is how I make my living."

Mama patted her hand. "Mrs. Hamilton, we're all in the same wagon."

Maria tried to concentrate on making the tea exactly as her mother had taught her. But her mind was on the adults' conversation as she put the tea into the water the moment it started boiling and let it steep.

She moved around the table leisurely pouring the tea, so that she could hear as much of their talk as possible. Mr. Francis smiled at her and then turned to Papa. "Your Maria is growing into a fine young lady." She felt a little guilty. *He doesn't know about the cuffing I gave his son,* she thought.

She glanced over at Moosa, who appeared to be bored and half asleep. She hoped that he'd drop off in the middle of everything and bang his head on the table.

How can he tell me what they discussed if he doesn't listen? she thought. *Papa should have asked me to sit with them.*

When she finished serving the tea, Maria stood at the oven and slowly wiped the top of the stove. Even after she'd taken up the last crumb, she kept on wiping. She heard Mr. Francis say, "If we make enough noise about this, someone might listen."

Suddenly Elizabeth raised her voice. "Simon! Stop that."

Mama called to Maria: "Go back there with the children, and keep them quiet."

Reluctantly, Maria walked to the far end of the sitting room. "What's wrong, Lizzie?" she asked.

"Simon is being contrary. And Diana is no help!"

Diana's eyes flashed as she put her hands on her hips. "I didn't do anything. We were playing, and . . ."

"I don't care what you were playing. Why can't you sit quietly until the meeting is over?"

"Well, what is the meeting about?"

"None of your business. You and Simon, write a poem; do something quiet," she ordered.

Diana crossed her arms in front of her. "You are so mean!"

"You'd better do as I say, Diana."

Diana stamped her foot and spun around, heading back toward the corner where she and Simon had been playing.

Maria wanted badly to go and stand by the stove again, but she didn't dare anger her mother. She sat at the far end of the sitting room and reluctantly picked up the socks she'd been knitting. Lizzie sat next to her, knitting a scarf. "She's angry with you, Maria."

"I don't care. I'm trying to hear what they're saying, and she can't keep quiet for a moment."

Simon and Diana sat at a small desk, giggling and talking quietly. "Well, I guess it's all forgotten. She's seems happy now," Elizabeth said, and then she turned to Maria. "Mama and Papa said not to worry, so why do you care what they're saying at the meeting?"

Maria sighed and rested her knitting in her lap. "Maybe you're right. Why do I need to know? I can't do anything to help anyway." Still, she gazed at them all sitting around the table and tried to hear something. She even tried to read the Magpie's chattering lips. She saw Farmer Gruner pick up his teacup, and it seemed to her that he held it to his mouth for such a long time it had to be the last sip. Maria put down her knitting, stood up, and walked over to the kitchen.

Mama was writing on a sheet of paper, and the Magpie was leaning over her shoulder. Moosa still seemed bored, and Papa looked up. "Maria, what is it?" he asked.

"I want to know whether anyone would like more tea?"

"Oh, yes," the Magpie said. "That would be wonderful."

Mr. Francis nodded, and Farmer Gruner said, "No, miss. I still have some left."

Mama said, "You can make another pot."

Maria made as little noise as possible as she filled the teapot with water. And as she waited for the water to boil she heard Papa say, "Read what we have so far, Catalina."

Mama read: *"To the Mayor, Alderman, and Commonalty of the City of New York: We are writing to you regarding the matter of purchasing our property for laying out a park between Fifty-ninth and 106th Streets. We, the undersigned, all own lots from Eighty-second to Eighty-ninth Streets between Seventh and Eighth Avenues. We are petitioning you to reconsider destroying our homes, church, and school buildings for a park."*

Maria's hand shook a little at the mention of their homes and school and church being destroyed. She almost missed putting the tea in the pot just as the water boiled.

Mama looked around. "How does that sound?"

Everyone agreed that it was fine.

Farmer Gruner supplied the next sentence: *"We want you should let us keep our property or pay for us what it's worth."*

The Magpie flicked her hand. "That's good, Farmer

Gruner. Catalina, write it this way: *"We want you to leave our property as it is or pay us its true value."*

Farmer Gruner rolled his eyes at the Magpie but said nothing.

Maria wanted to the tell the Magpie that her neck would break if she kept leaning over Mama that way.

Mama continued reading: *"All of us have owned homes here for sixteen years and more. Our children attend school here, and if we are forced to move, our children will not be able to go to school, as there are only two other schools for colored students in this city. Our dead are also buried here, in the African Methodist Episcopal Zion Church cemetery."*

Maria walked around the table and refilled the teacups, including Farmer Gruner's.

Mama kept reading: *"As you know, land is very dear in this city. If we cannot get a fair value for our homes, we surely will not be able to purchase another roof to place over our families' heads. Losing our property, without being fairly compensated for same, would cause us extreme hardship."*

The Magpie stood up when Mama finished reading. "Very nice, very nice. The city fathers should take notice."

They signed and dated the petition. Papa put his arm around Moosa's shoulders.

"Tomorrow you'll go to the other neighbors and get their signatures."

"We'll all help," the Magpie offered.

When everyone had left, Papa plopped down in his chair. "I'm tired."

He called out to Mama, who was helping Maria clear

the table. "So now, we'll see what happens," he said.

Mama turned to Maria as she took the teacups into the kitchen, "Thank you, Maria. You were a good help," she said.

"Let me help Moosa get the signatures."

"No. You've done enough. You have to go to school."

"I just wanted to help, too."

"You've already helped, my sweet."

Maria began washing the cups and saucers in the large tin pan. "Mama, what will happen if the city still takes the property?"

Mama sighed. "Then we'll have to move. Papa has been talking about Kansas, maybe. But don't worry yourself. How was school today?"

"Papa!" Diana shouted, "Simon has a poem to tell you." She ran into the kitchen.

"Maria, Mama, everybody! Come and hear it."

"I have to finish the dishes," Maria said.

"You're the one who told me to do it," Diana said.

Mama gave Maria a little push. "Go on and listen to her poem. She's so excited. I'll finish the dishes." Maria walked reluctantly into the sitting room. She had a feeling she'd be sorry she'd told Diana to write a poem.

CHAPTER 12

IN TROUBLE

EVERYONE ONE ELSE was sitting, even Moosa, as if they were watching a show. But Maria remained near the kitchen with her arms folded. Papa's eyes were practically closed. "Go on, children. I need some entertainment this evening." His smile seemed strained.

Simon bowed, placing one arm across his waist and the other behind his back, as if he were on a stage. Diana stood next to him, grinning. He began.

> *Maria likes to fight.*
> *She hit a boy with all her might.*
> *The boy fell down and has a lump on his*
> *   crown.*
> *Why does Maria love to fight,*
> *hitting a boy with all of her might?*

Then he proclaimed, "This is about Maria, who was bad in school today."

Maria almost snatched him by his britches. Diana doubled over laughing, and Mama dropped her knitting needles. "Stop it!" she shouted.

Elizabeth looked surprised. Papa looked puzzled. "What's the matter? I like the poem. It's not about our Maria, is it? Maybe you should change the girl's name."

Maria stared at Diana, who was still giggling. "Papa, the poem is about me. I hit Byron because he made fun of me. I'm sorry, Papa," Maria said.

"He didn't hit you first?"

"No," she said, lowering her head.

"Well, you were wrong, then. You weren't defending yourself."

Mama wagged her finger at Maria. "I told you about fighting. Now I'll have to contend with his mother complaining to me. Maria, how can you be so grown up on one hand and so childish on the other?" Then she said just the thing Maria didn't want to hear: "No trip downtown on Saturday."

"Mama," Moosa said, "Maria didn't mean to do anything wrong. Byron shouldn't be insulting her. Let her go with us on Saturday. She's just fiery. "

"That's not a good way for a young lady to be," Mama said. "Fighting like a street urchin."

"You have to learn how to control your fire," Papa said staring at her. "Maria, your mother is right. You have to learn how to act like a young lady at all times."

Diana had a self-satisfied look on her face until her father called her and Simon over to him. "Stop teasing your sister."

"You're wicked and evil," Maria whispered to Diana before they climbed into bed that night.

Elizabeth, who, luckily, slept between them, said, "Hush. It's over now. We're still sisters."

Maria turned her back on them both.

She's not my sister anymore, she thought.

The next morning, Maria woke up without her mother's help. The room was freezing, as usual, but she was still on fire from the night before. Just hearing Diana snore angered her.

She listened for her mother's voice, but the house was still. Quickly and quietly, she washed her face and arms in the basin. Then, shivering, she put on her school dress and apron. She brushed the top and sides of her hair and tightened her one long thick braid.

Her sisters slept so soundly that Maria was able to use the chamber pot in their bedroom, rather than having to go to the privy outside. Then she heard her parents talking quietly in their bedroom. What were they talking about? The petition? Moving away? Or were they talking about her?

The whole house would be stirring soon. She treasured the few moments she'd be alone with her own thoughts, pretending that she could do whatever she wanted to do, in her own imagination at least.

She carried the chamber pot downstairs, walking through the pantry, the laundry and storage room, and then a few steps outside to the privy, where she dumped the pot. She entered and exited the icy privy quickly, taking a glance beyond the bare trees to see a ribbon of light. Her mother had told them when they were little that God was slowly opening His window to let His light shine on the world. Maria was never afraid of the darkness of dawn after that.

She carried the pot back upstairs to the bedroom, quickly sliding it under the bed and leaving the room. As she tiptoed back downstairs she heard her parents still talking and Moosa stirring in the bedroom he shared with Simon.

The embers burned dully in the fireplace, barely noticeable among the ashes. She threw in several logs and watched the fire blaze, giving warmth and light to the cold, dark sitting room. She then went to the front hallway, put on her boots, cloak, and gloves and picked up the two pails. As she was leaving, she heard her mother calling in a screechy voice, "Wake-up time, girls, wake up, lazybones."

Maria opened the door and left the house. Dukie raced out ahead of her. She appreciated the company of her dog. Dogs did not tell secrets. They did not scold. The ribbon of light was changing shape. Now it was a square, like a window, with pink light showing through it. Maria felt as comfortable as if it were bright daylight. No one could scold her now. She'd started her chores before everyone else. After filling her pails with the icy water, she walked across Cedar Lane and saw Moosa standing in the doorway.

"Why are you out here so early, and why did you go alone?" He looked down at Dukie. "Guess you weren't really alone." Moosa took the full pails from Maria and placed them in the entryway. "I'll help you with the other ones," he said. He picked up two empty pails. "Maria, don't look so miserable. Mama and Papa may change their minds and let you go on Saturday. I'll talk to them."

Maria threw her head back and raised her chin. "I'm going to talk to them, too. That fight was just a small thing, Moosa."

"Not to Byron, it wasn't," he smiled. They stepped over some dried twigs and startled several squirrels.

"I wish I could take the petition around with you. Do you think everyone will sign it?"

"I think so. Most people want to stay in the village."

"Except you."

"Well, I'm not most people," Moosa said as they walked toward a stand of bare oak trees.

They could see the smoke rising from Reverend Arlington's home as they crossed Cedar Lane and walked toward the stream. The few pine trees were green, but the rest of the trees and bushes were still gray and brown and bare. But, Maria thought, there was beauty in the way the branches reached out and the vines and brambles twisted and wound their way around one another. Moosa and

Maria dipped their pails into the stream.

"I don't know why Papa is doing all of this. He should take whatever money the city gives him, and then we could all move west," Moosa said.

"Why don't you like it here? I do."

"There's adventure and real freedom out there. Not to mention gold." He dipped his other pail in the water. "You know, Mama is right when she talks about kidnappers. There's kidnappers snatching up free coloreds to sell in the South. There's runaway slaves all over the city, and slave-catchers looking for them."

"You never tell Mama she's right."

Moosa finished filling the pail and stood up. "If I tell her she's right she'll worry herself sick. So I try to ease her mind."

"There's no slavery in the West?"

"No. You won't have to carry papers to show you're free out there."

"But Papa wants you to be a doctor or a lawyer."

"Even if I do learn to be a doctor or a lawyer, where would I practice? Who would hire me? The doctor business is Papa's dream. Not mine. I'm leaving here someday."

She stood up, noticing that the morning sky was growing lighter. She thought about Miss Truth. "But maybe we should stay here and fight. Miss Truth says *we* have the power to free the slaves. Remember when she pointed at each of us in church?"

Moosa looked at Maria with a playful twinkle in his eyes. "You are a fighter. I'm going to tell Mama and Papa that you need to come to the meetings and join the anti-slavery society."

"You don't think I'm serious, do you, Moosa?"

"I know you're serious, and so does Byron. I hear that he has a lump as big as a melon on the side of his head."

Maria grinned. "You heard no such thing."

As they neared Cedar Lane they could see smoke curling out of most of the chimneys of the homes along the road. When they entered the house, Mama was in the kitchen. "Good morning, my sweets," she said in her cheery voice.

"It's so nice and warm in here. Moosa, you started the fire early."

"Maria did it. She was the first one up this morning."

"Oh, my sweet. Thank you."

Maria's heart felt light at that moment. Maybe Mama wasn't as angry as she'd thought. "Mama, do you want me to make the wheat cakes?"

"Yes. Please." She looked up at the ceiling. "I don't hear your sisters moving around. Let me make sure they're up."

She turned to leave, and Maria said, "Mama, I'm sorry for fighting. Can I please go with Moosa and Papa on Saturday?"

"No, Maria. I'm not going back on my word. You have to learn how to control your temper. I thought that you and Byron were friends."

"We were until he made fun of me."

"That's no excuse, Maria. That's the way a child thinks. I'm sorry. You cannot go on Saturday."

CHAPTER 13

A GOOD DEED

A S MARIA AND HER SISTERS walked down Cedar Lane, the air was still crisp and cold, but sunny. Diana inserted herself between Maria and Elizabeth instead of running off with her friends. She chirped like a little cricket. "We're going to have sewing all day. The examinations start tomorrow. I hope we pass."

"Oh, I'm sure we'll pass," Elizabeth said patiently.

Maria was silent. She caught a glimpse of Little Miss, rushing down the hill.

A group of boys passed them once they reached the cedar grove and the Magpie's house. They darted back and forth, hitting and shouting at each other on their way to school. Byron was among them, but he looked the other way when he saw the girls.

"Those boys all have pointy heads," Diana said,

peeping at Maria, who stared straight ahead as they walked. Elizabeth laughed.

Maria was silent the rest of the way to school.

The sisters lined up with the other students. Diana ran to the front of the line with the younger girls, and Elizabeth remained nearby. Maria spotted Anna in her oversize cloak, talking to a few of the older girls in the middle of the line. Before she could walk over to her, Miss James came outside, and everyone had to stand in their places. It was still a strange sight to see Anna towering over the little ABC girls in the front of the line.

Miss James stood before the whole school in one of her perfect black dresses, with a collar trimmed in white lace that she herself had made, in class, when she gave the boring tatting lessons. "Girls, as you know, we have a lot of work to do before Friday's examinations. Those of you who have not completed your sewing projects have only today and tomorrow to sew."

Maria thought that Miss James looked straight at her.

"Let me remind you that I do not want to see a hairpin or a hem out of place on Examination Day. Make sure you are squeaky-clean young ladies—especially the parts of your body we can see. Your hair, face, and nails." Some of the girls giggled.

"I'm not joking, young ladies. Cleanliness is next to godliness."

Maria leaned over to Sarah. "Then some of these girls are full of the devil," she whispered.

Their morning routine passed as usual: Bible verses, spelling, geography, then math. Anna was writing on her slate, and Maria wondered whether her letter *B* was still crooked. Maria had expected that after the spelling lesson, Miss James would call on her to help Anna. But she didn't.

When their multiplication practice was almost over, Miss James made an announcement. "Girls, for the rest of the day and all day tomorrow, we'll concentrate on completing our sewing projects."

At lunchtime Maria stayed inside. The clear, crisp, sunny morning gave way to a gray, freezing afternoon. She didn't want to have another fight with Byron, so she ate lunch with Elizabeth and Anna.

When the lunch recess ended, the girls took their sewing baskets out of the closet. The samplers, aprons, dresses, embroidery, and purses decorated with beads and shells filled the room with color as the girls worked on their sewing projects.

Maria dreaded a whole afternoon of sewing. She'd rather have taught Anna the alphabet. But she was determined to do better with her sewing so that she could become a monitor. As soon as Maria took her sewing basket out of the closet, Miss James called her to the front of the room. Maria quickly walked over to the teacher's desk.

"Maria, did you take the shirt apart as I'd asked?"

"Yes, Miss James," she said, confident that Anna had

taken out the stitches for her. She slowly opened her basket in front of Miss James and thought that her eyes had deceived her.

The shirt was whole, perfectly sewn together. It had been washed and ironed and was sparkling white. Every stitch was strong and straight.

Miss James held up the shirt. "Maria, when did you do this? You took it home and Elizabeth did it for you."

All activity in the room stopped. Someone whispered loudly, "Maria is working magic."

"I don't want to hear any comments from any of you unless you raise your hand to speak," Miss James said. She shook her head, her face grave and serious. The lines around her lips deepened, as they always did when she was upset.

"Miss James, Elizabeth didn't fix my shirt," Maria said.

Looking upset, Elizabeth raised her hand. "Miss James, I didn't sew Maria's shirt."

It seemed as if Miss James had not heard them. "Maria, this is so dishonest; and I'm surprised at you, Elizabeth. I know your mother has no idea what you girls were up to." Her voice rose.

"No, Miss James. Elizabeth didn't do it," Maria repeated.

Elizabeth was practically in tears. "Miss James, I didn't sew it for her."

As she'd seen the other students do, Anna raised her hand and smiled innocently and sweetly. "Miz James, I sew the shirt."

"You did this?"

"Yes, ma'am, Miz James." She smiled proudly.

Miss James looked at the shirt in disbelief.

"When?"

"I took it home, to help Maria."

"Maria, this is wrong. You're not supposed to let someone else do your work. You took advantage of Anna."

"But, Miss James, she offered to take out the stitches for me because I was helping her with her letters. I didn't know that she was going to sew the whole shirt."

Still holding the shirt, Miss James stood up. "Both of you, come to my office." Maria didn't have to look in order to know that every girl stared at her and Anna as they followed Miss James out of the classroom.

It was only a short walk to Miss James's small office. She motioned for Maria and Anna to sit down.

"Anna, you really did this? Your mother or someone else didn't help you?"

"No, ma'am, Miz James. No one help me."

Maria noticed that Miss James forgot to correct the *ma'am*'s.

"We always sew. We make everything. My mama take in laundry, so she wash and iron it."

Miss James stared at her in disbelief. "Explain how you made it. What's the first step and the next and so on?"

Anna picked up the shirt. "First, I sew the wristband, before the sleeve is made. Then I hem the sleeve on each side."

"How much do you hem?"

"A finger length, ma'am. I mean, Miz James. Then

I gather it and sew real strong. I smooth the gathering with small stitches. Then I do the linings with big, loose stitches."

"Basting stitches," Miss James said.

"Yes, ma'am. Then I sew the side and put in the sleeve. I take three threads and whip it around the buttonholes, like so." She demonstrated how she made the stitches one over the other to finish off the buttonholes.

"You really do know how to sew. I don't blame you, Anna, because you didn't know better, but we never take sewing work home; it is completed in class. Maria should not have let you take the shirt home. I understand why you wanted to help her, because she's been nice to you. But you cannot do her work for her. Do you understand?"

"Yes, ma'am." Anna lowered her head.

Miss James turned to Maria. "You will not get a sewing grade at all." She handed her the shirt. "You will take it apart again."

"But, Miss James, it's so perfect."

"Yes, but you didn't perfect it. You will keep at this until you get it right; otherwise there's no point in your being in school." The teacher took a breath before continuing her lecture. "The sewing class is the most important class for you girls. What kind of mother will you be? Why, you'll have naked children scampering around your feet, because you can't make their clothing. Even the little girls are sewing. Every woman has to be able to sew and do needlework."

Maria wondered whether that was in the Bible, that

women had to sew. Her father had told them that every good and right thing that people must do was in there. She looked at the floor. As angry as she felt, the image of naked children running around her feet amused her. Anna showed no emotion, just kept her head bowed, but Maria thought she saw her smile a little.

Miss James started to turn red as she stared at Maria. "You will spend the rest of the afternoon taking those stitches out. And you will not participate in the multiplication demonstration." She patted Anna on the shoulder. "Anna, I'll let you make a sampler. Then you'll get a sewing grade. I'm sure you'll be able to do it by Friday."

Anna returned to her desk, and Miss James sent Maria to the table in the hallway. Maria slowly and torturously pulled Anna's strong, tight, perfect stitches out of the shirt.

An afternoon became an eternity.

By the time the church bells sounded five times, Maria had taken the stitches apart. She walked back to the classroom and put her sewing basket, with the undone shirt in it, back in the closet.

Elizabeth and Anna were waiting for her.

"Wait for me outside," Maria said. "I'm going to talk to Miss James and try to explain what happened."

"You already explained," Elizabeth said.

"I have to convince her that I didn't mean to do anything wrong."

Anna looked upset. "I get you in trouble. I'm sorry. I didn't know."

"It's not your fault, Anna. You were just trying to help me."

She left them and walked to Miss James's office. The door was wide open, but when she looked in she was shocked. The Magpie was sitting there moving her head back and forth and waving her hands. Maria stepped away from the door quickly, before they saw her, and ran back down the hallway. She didn't want Miss James to say anything to her about the shirt in front of the Magpie. And what was Mrs. Hamilton doing in Miss James's office, anyway?

When she got outside, Anna was just walking out of the school yard. Elizabeth was waiting, standing close to the building trying to protect herself from the icy rain. Diana had already started walking up the hill with her friends.

"What happened? You talked that fast?" Elizabeth asked. Maria explained.

They left the school yard, and Maria caught a glimpse of Anna and her mother walking down the hill. Maria wondered why Anna's mother was still meeting her every day after school, but she thought no more of it as she and Elizabeth huddled together, hurrying up Cedar Lane.

"I wonder why the Magpie was visiting Miss James," Elizabeth said. "Why do you think, Maria?"

"I don't know. Maybe she was telling Miss James about the petition."

"Where does Anna live?"

Elizabeth shrugged her shoulders. "I'm not sure. But I've seen her walking up the hill to school."

Maria could still see Diana walking with her friends. "Do you think Miss James will tell Headmaster Clark what you did?" Elizabeth asked.

Maria lowered her head to avoid the stinging rain. "She doesn't always tell him everything that happens in the girls' school. And stop thinking about the worst thing that could happen, Lizzie."

"How do you know what she tells the headmaster?" Elizabeth asked as they passed Little Miss's house.

"She punishes us herself."

They waved at Mrs. Francis, who was rushing to her house as it began to sleet harder.

"Oh, Lizzie, what can I do now? I thought I could talk to Miss James."

"Maybe you should just tell Mama what happened."

"I can't, Lizzie. She'll never let me go anywhere. Do you know how angry she'll be over this shirt?"

"Maybe she'll understand if you tell her first."

Maria shook her head. "She won't. She'll say the same thing Miss James said. My only hope is that Miss James won't walk up this hill and won't see Mama until Sunday in church. If she doesn't know about the shirt, she still might change her mind about letting me go with Moosa and Papa to the meeting." She looked around and saw Diana racing ahead of them. Simon and Dukie weren't outside to meet them this afternoon. Before Diana rounded the corner to Mama's store, Maria called to her.

Diana ran back to her with a wide smile on her face, as if she were glad Maria was finally talking to her.

"You better not wag your long clack tongue to Mama about me sitting in the hallway all afternoon. Otherwise, I'll never speak to you again."

"Don't talk to her so mean," Elizabeth said softly.

Diana's large eyes welled up with tears. "I won't," she said, and she slipped off again.

"You hurt her feelings," Elizabeth said.

"She hurt mine, too, and purposely got me in trouble. And I'll be in worse trouble if she runs her mouth to Mama about the shirt."

CHAPTER 14

PREPARATIONS

VEN IF DIANA had wanted to tell her mother about
Maria's troubles in school, it would have been
impossible. When Maria entered the store, the first
person she saw was Moosa, standing with a crowd of
other people—Mr. Davis, Little Miss's father; Mrs.
Francis; and several men who lived in the neighborhood.
Simon ran over to Maria. "Moosa is home! And we have a
lot of company in the store!"

"Yes, Simon, I see." She was relieved, knowing that the
great crowd of people in the store had nothing to do with
her. Her mother was smiling and holding the petition as
Moosa stood over her.

"Oh, here they are now," Mama said excitedly when
the girls walked in.

"What happened, Mama?" Diana blurted out. "Why

are so many people in the store?"

Mama laid the petition on the counter and kissed Diana on the top of the head.

"Go to the cellar and bring a dozen eggs and five potatoes. Simon, help your sister."

"But I want to take my reading lesson with Maria."

"You'll get your lesson later. Maria has something to do now."

"Something to do?"

Diana rolled her eyes in Maria's direction as Elizabeth gently pushed her to the back of the store.

Mama said to Elizabeth, "Make us some tea, my sweet."

Maria wondered what was going on. Moosa winked at her and grinned from ear to ear, so Maria decided that whatever it was couldn't be bad. Then he said to Mama, "I'm going to meet Papa now at the Eighth Avenue depot."

"Maria, take off your coat; get comfortable; we need you to write another petition just like the first one."

"She can write so well?" Mr. Davis asked.

"Yes," Moosa said, "she has a perfect hand."

Mama hung up Maria's coat on the rack. "Maria, Moosa got so many signatures today, and we didn't have enough space for the signatures of our neighbors here. So we need you to write the same letter again."

"We need at least two more letters," Mr. Davis said. "Everyone wants to sign."

Maria was no longer worried as she painstakingly copied the petition twice.

Suddenly the bells jangled loudly as the Magpie burst into the store.

"She'll do it!" the Magpie shouted. Maria almost made a great ink blot on the page.

Mama smiled. "I knew she'd help us."

"What's this?" one of the men asked.

"Well, some of us who met last night wanted to make sure that the right people presented the petition at City Hall," Mama said.

Mrs. Hamilton interrupted. "In other words, we need respectable-looking people. Miss James looks like a white lady. Otherwise, those thieves in City Hall will throw us out and tear up our petition as soon as we leave."

Mrs. Hamilton tilted her head to one side and continued as if she were the leader of the petitioners. "We thought it best to have a real proper looking and sounding lady to go to City Hall with the petition. And Solomon Peters, Mr. Davis here, and Reverend Arlington will go with her, because they are freeholders and qualify to vote."

"Farmer Gruner qualifies to vote, I think," Mr. Davis said. "He's been living in America for over three years."

"Well, he can go to if he wants to, but he shouldn't speak, because he sounds like he just came off the boat," Mrs. Hamilton said, and then she sat down at the small table next to Maria, who tried to concentrate and not pay attention to the Magpie.

Diana and Simon returned from the cellar with the eggs and potatoes, and Mama sent them into the house.

Elizabeth brought out the tea, and Mama cut a few slices of cheese for one of her customers while Maria worked on copying the petitions.

She completed one copy, and Mr. Davis and the other men signed. Even two of Mama's customers who hadn't seen the first petition signed it. Maria blocked out the Magpie's chatter and began to copy the second petition.

Maria's penmanship was perfect as she carefully copied the words. Her long face had softened, and she looked peaceful as she formed the letters of the document that would perhaps save their homes.

Mama said, "I'm so proud of my Maria."

"Oh, yes," the Magpie agreed, "presentation is of the essence. If those letters are misspelled and sloppily written, do you think the clerk would even try to read them? Into the trash they would go. She sat there like a little lady and didn't make one mistake in her writing."

Maria didn't worry anymore about Miss James walking up the hill that evening. First of all, it was too late, and second, her mother seemed so proud of her now that she'd probably forgive the mistake with Anna. Maria felt as if a weight had been lifted from her. Now, if Diana could keep her clack tongue quiet, all would be fine, and Mama might change her mind and let her go to the meeting on Saturday.

Mama stopped folding and putting away the handkerchiefs and socks she'd had on display, and turned to Maria. "You can do Simon's lessons with him. I'll close up the shop."

Maria walked to the back of the store and into the house. Elizabeth looked up from chopping onions with Diana. "What did Mama want you to do?"

Maria explained; she wondered what devilment was spinning around in Diana's head. But, as if reading her mind, Diana, while continuing to chop an onion, said, "I won't tell Mama that Miss James made you stay in the hallway all afternoon because Anna did your sewing."

"You'd better not," Maria said. She called Simon over and they sat down at the kitchen table, along with Diana and Elizabeth. While she pronounced and pointed out words to him, her thoughts turned once again to Saturday, and to wondering how she could possibly get her mother to change her mind and let her go.

She glanced out of the window and noticed a light snowfall. After Mama closed the store, she started preparing a roast chicken for their supper. The clock struck once, and Maria saw that it was seven thirty. A few moments later, Dukie ran to the door with his stubby tail wagging furiously. Papa and Moosa were in the yard.

Maria never got the chance to talk to her mother alone. Papa looked very calm as he patted Moosa on the back and said, "Son, you did a wonderful job. Every property owner in the village signed."

Maria waited for him to say something about how nicely she had copied the additional petitions. But before he could say anything else, Diana began to question him.

"So we won't have to move, Papa?" she asked.

Papa frowned. "Who told you about moving?"

"Amy and the other girls in my form."

"Well, don't listen to what you hear. It's nothing for you to worry about."

"Yes, Papa."

Mama sliced the chicken. "Girls, now all I want you to think about is the big day tomorrow. You should pass your examinations easily."

Diana instantly seemed to forget whatever she had heard about moving. Her eyes sparkled as she talked about her sewing project for school.

"You girls should take your baths tonight," Mama said.

"Are you going to put some rose water in our baths, Mama?" Diana asked.

"Yes, my sweet."

Maria smiled. It was a special treat to have Mama's perfume in their bathwater. *Mama is trying to make our lives sweet,* she thought.

The next morning, the house buzzed with activity.

The girls were told they did not have to do their regular morning chores. Mama had made them identical burgundy-colored woolen dresses with white buttons going up the front. She'd also made them new white aprons that sparkled. The aprons reminded Maria of her shirt, which Anna had sewn, cleaned, and ironed to perfection.

Mama made sure that their hair was brushed, with every strand in place. She gave each of them a piece of clove, so that their breath would smell good.

"Someone might talk directly to you. Bad breath makes a bad impression, girls."

Maria and Moosa had a chance to talk as they put on their coats and boots. She told him what Anna had done.

"Sister, that is so funny."

"Funny?"

"Yes, it's ridiculous and funny." He tied his heavy brogans. "But that girl is a true friend to you. You're lucky to have a friend who'd do that for you—even though it got you in trouble. See how ridiculous that is?"

Maria saw it, and she suddenly was tickled, too. So much so that even though she had never liked Examination Day, she smiled to herself all the way to school.

CHAPTER 15

EXAMINATION DAY

THE EXAMINERS WERE already there when the children arrived. There were twenty visitors, two of them wearing clergymen's collars. It was strange to Maria and the other children to see so many white faces all at once at the school. Only one of the clergymen smiled at them.

How she hated the examinations. She felt like an object on display when the solemn-faced white men on the school board made sure that they were being taught properly and that they were learning their lessons.

Headmaster Clark and Miss James looked as solemn as the school board. The students quietly lined up before them and marched into the boys' building. This was one of the rare times the boys and girls would be grouped together. Examinations and special programs were always held in the auditorium of the boys' school, since the girls' building did not have an auditorium.

The boys quietly hung their outer clothing in the closet and took their seats, and the girls were orderly as they filed into the auditorium and gave their cloaks and scarves to the monitors, who hung them up for them in the girls' building. They did not make a sound.

Colored School Number Three was perfection on Examination Day. Everything sparkled. The windows gleamed, and the polished floors shone. The newly white-washed walls were blinding. Even the children were freshly scrubbed—nails clipped, every hair in place, and every button and seam lined up just so. Even those who usually always had to be reminded to keep their hands and nails clean and their hair brushed were neatly dressed that morning. The sun didn't shine any brighter than the students did on Examination Day.

The boys' woolen trousers were clean, and they all wore white shirts. Some of them wore suits—with waist-high trousers and fitted jackets. A few wore breeches that ended below their knees. Some old-fashioned people still believed that a man or boy was not formally dressed unless he wore breeches.

Some girls had only one dress to wear to school every day, but that one dress was clean on this occasion. Anna did not wear her usual school dress—instead she had on a black velvet dress with burgundy-colored ruffles around the wrists and hem. It seemed too old for a girl to wear.

Maria noticed, though, that Anna's boots were still

scuffed and the heels worn, and she felt sorry for Anna. The fancy dress didn't match the boots. Maria wished she could take them to her father. He would make them shine like a mirror. Anna would be able to see her own reflection in them.

The examiners sat on chairs placed on the stage. A large blackboard in a wooden frame stood there, too. The boys sat on one side of the auditorium and the girls on the other; Miss James, arms folded, stood near the girls' section, and Headmaster Clark hovered over the boys.

Byron was the first student to make a presentation. It was all Maria could do to keep from giggling aloud. She heard a faint snicker as he stepped up to the stage. Headmaster Clark and Miss James heard it, too. They both stiffened and looked as though they were ready to rush toward the offending student.

Byron wore tight breeches and was the only boy in the whole school wearing a ruffled shirt. He still had the lump on his forehead, which Maria thought did not match his fancy shirt. He stood very straight and held his head up proudly as he recited the opening speech.

"Respected Gentlemen, Headmaster Clark, Miss James, and fellow students, it becomes my duty to commence these exercises," he said in a loud voice, pronouncing each word precisely, as Headmaster Clark had trained him to do. The headmaster had written the speech for Byron, who had memorized it. "If we had been born in the southern section of our country, it would have been against the law for us to learn how to read and write. . . ."

Maria had to fold her hands and purse her lips tightly in order to keep a straight face. Byron was pronouncing his words so properly he sounded like a hoot owl. Instead of listening to him, she watched the reaction of the examiners. The same clergyman who'd smiled at them before now beamed at Byron. The other examiners watched and listened to Byron's performance with serious faces, but Maria thought one or two of them looked a little amused.

Byron, appearing pleased with himself, continued to hold his head high as he stepped off the stage. Unfortunately, this caused him to stumble. Maria was sure that she had heard his breeches rip. The headmaster whisked him out of the auditorium so fast that Maria thought he must have put some kind of spell on the poor boy to make him disappear.

Maria watched as one group of girls after another presented their subjects to the examiners. As Maria's group demonstrated their multiplication skills, Maria regretted that she was barred from participating. She could have dazzled the examiners. Twice, the girl who replaced her gave an incorrect answer, which had to be corrected by another girl. Had Maria been involved, that would never have happened.

The geography demonstration was next, followed by the presentations by the members of the Boys' Class of Merit, who studied navigation and astronomy.

Diana made the final presentation. She stepped onto the stage looking like a little doll in her burgundy dress.

She'd taken off her apron; and made a bright flower out of red paper, which she pinned to the waist of her dress. Maria noticed that Miss James frowned a little, which meant that Diana had made these changes without asking anyone's permission.

Diana curtsied to the audience and then to the examiners, just as Miss James had told her not to do. A few of the examiners actually smiled, but Miss James's lip was twitching again. As Maria watched her little sister, looking so brave in front of such a large audience, she found herself hoping that she would perform well. Her heart softened. Diana was her little sister, after all.

As she spoke, Diana's voice rang out loud and clear.

> *Praise of Creation,*
> *by George Horton*
>
> *Creation fires my tongue!*
> *Nature, thy anthems raise,*
> *And spread the universal song*
> *Of thy Creator's praise. . . .*

Maria could hardly listen to the rest of the poem. She closed her eyes and prayed that Diana wouldn't forget her lines.

As she finished, Diana made another curtsy to the examiners and the audience, and the applause was loud; maybe that was why she also twirled this time. All twenty examiners smiled at her as she skipped off the stage. Miss

James's lip stopped twitching, but Maria noticed that drops of sweat were forming on her forehead.

Finally, the examiners went into the boys' classroom, where the shirts, ties, dresses, samplers, and other items the girls had made were displayed. Miss James seemed to be in her glory as she walked from table to table with the examiners in tow.

All of the students had to remain sitting quietly in the auditorium with the monitors, as the examiners inspected the girls' sewing work. But when the last of the examiners had left the auditorium to walk to their waiting carriages, the children erupted in chatter.

Headmaster Clark stood before the entire student body, smiling for the first time that year. "Boys and girls," he said, "we did it. The examiners were impressed! You were, each and every one of you, wonderful! One of the good reverends said to me that he has never seen students, white or black, perform so superbly. You have brought honor to our school, boys and girls. Now, if all of you will help clean up, you can have lunch and a free afternoon."

Everyone cheered, even Maria, who felt that she wasn't a part of anything.

CHAPTER 16

A GREAT SUCCESS

EVEN THE SUN seemed to smile on them that afternoon, giving a hint of spring.

The younger girls in Diana's form immediately started playing I Spy.

A bunch of boys played leapfrog, jumping over one another.

"Come on, Maria," one of the girls shouted. "Play Wash My Lady's Dresses with us. You, too, Anna; we'll show you how."

Out of the corner of her eye, though, Maria saw Byron and five other boys playing Touch. Byron wasn't wearing the fancy breeches anymore, but a regular pair of trousers. She shook her head. "Anna and I don't feel like playing that. We're going to play Touch."

"What's that?" Anna asked.

"It's so much fun. Can you run?"

"Yes. I run fast."

"Watch us." Maria ran over to the boys. "I want to play, too," she said to them.

"You can't play. You're a girl."

"She'll cuff you if you don't let her play," one of the boys laughed.

"I'll beat you up if you don't let me play!" she shouted. "I'll be Touch."

"You'll be out in a minute!" a boy hollered as he grinned in her face.

Anna seemed fascinated as she watched Maria play the game.

She chased all of the boys and in no time touched one of the slower ones. He became Touch and chased after Maria first, but gave up when he couldn't catch her. In the meantime, Maria caught up to Byron, who ran even faster. "I'm sorry!" she yelled after him. He didn't answer, but she was certain that he'd heard her.

Suddenly, Anna left the group of boys and girls cheering the players on and joined the game. She ran even faster than Maria, as the boy who was Touch came after her.

A large senior boy won the game, but he said to Maria and Anna, "You girls play as good as boys."

"Thank you," they both said proudly.

Maria and Anna played I Spy with a group of girls in Elizabeth's form and then watched the boys playing ball. Even Miss James and Headmaster Clark came outside and watched the game, smiling the whole time. Maria forgot about the possibility of Miss James's coming to inform her mother that she'd failed her sewing examination.

As a pink line of color spread over the western sky and the buildings off in the distance, the games and the racing and running slowed. The children finally dispersed.

Anna smiled and waved to Maria as she walked down the hill. As usual, Anna's mother was waiting to meet her. As Maria headed up toward home, she remembered her fear that Miss James might come tell her mother about the shirt.

But as she looked back, she saw that Miss James was walking in the opposite direction.

She turned to Elizabeth as they passed Little Miss's house. Mr. Davis was putting his horse in the stable.

"Miss James isn't coming to tell Mama about the shirt," Maria said. "She's going to wait until Sunday. I'm going to ask Mama again if I can go to the meeting with Moosa and Papa tomorrow."

"Why do you want to go?" Elizabeth asked.

"It will be interesting, and I want to hear the discussions. Maybe Miss Truth will be there."

Elizabeth frowned. "Discussions don't sound so interesting to me. You should tell Mama what happened."

Maria didn't answer her, because she knew that Elizabeth was right. Mrs. Hamilton was outside, on the porch of her boarding house, talking with Mrs. Francis.

Maria said, "I bet the Magpie is on her way to Mama's store."

"Maria!" she heard Byron shout behind her. He caught

up and walked alongside her. "I accept your apology," he said, and raced up the steps to his house.

When the girls neared their home, Dukie and Simon ran out to meet them. Then they all, including Dukie, ran around the back to Mama's store. Diana burst in first, almost knocking down a customer who was leaving. With eyes flashing and hands waving excitedly, she told her mother everything that had happened.

Mama was folding socks. "Diana," Mama said, "calm down. You're not letting your sisters get a word in. Maria, how did your group do in multiplication? Were all of your answers correct?"

"Well, I . . ."

Diana interrupted. "Oh, Mama, Maria is tops in ciphering." She described Byron's ripped breeches.

"And Lizzie, how about your group? Did you answer all of your questions correctly?"

"Oh, yes. It was the best my group has ever done."

"And Mama, this is how I said my poem," Diana bragged, demonstrating the way she had twirled and curtsied when she recited it. Simon imitated her movements.

Mama laughed and was so entertained she didn't question Maria about her presentation. Maria realized that Diana had diverted their mother's attention. Maria's heart, again, softened toward her sister.

"I am so proud of you girls." Mama kissed each of them, and Maria felt sure that she could convince her mother to let her go to the meeting the next day. A customer walked in asking to buy a pair of socks for a child.

Mama took out the display case, and Diana and Elizabeth went into the house to begin supper.

Simon pulled Maria's skirt. "Where's my reading lesson?"

As Maria sat at the table in the store, listening to Simon read, she reviewed in her mind how she would approach her mother about going to the meeting on Saturday. Other people came into the store; one lady bought a pound of sugar, and another, several eggs. The Magpie rushed in, talking as always. They all lingered, talking softly.

By the time Simon finished his lesson and ran back to the house, the women had also left. Maria refilled the sugar jar and said, "Mama, I'm sorry about hitting Byron. I know it was childish, and I'll never do such a thing again." She hesitated a moment. "I apologized to him, and he accepted."

Mama stopped dusting the counter and looked Maria squarely in the eye. "You want to be treated like a young lady? Well, you have to act like one."

The memory of the way she had ripped and roared with the boys that afternoon made Maria feel a little ashamed. Remembering the shirt brought still more shame, and she realized that she should tell her mother, before Miss James did, that she had not even participated in the Examination Day demonstrations. But she couldn't open her mouth. She bowed her head so that her mother couldn't continue to look into her eyes.

"Another thing, Maria: as I told you before, these

meetings are a serious business. You're not to go there just to be entertained and get out of doing your work. Or to follow behind Moosa." She carefully laid out some new suspenders in one of the display cases. "You did a wonderful job copying the petitions, and your examinations went well, but I'm not letting you go tomorrow night."

"But, Mama, tomorrow is my birthday. And that's all I want." She leaned in toward her mother, the way she always did when she was in an excited state. "Please, Mama?"

"Maria, you have to pay when you do something wrong. I want you to understand this lesson, so that you don't make even bigger mistakes when you grow older."

"Yes, Mama," Maria said, staring at the ground.

Tomorrow would not be a happy birthday.

CHAPTER 17

MARIA'S BIRTHDAY

HE FIRST THING Maria did on the morning of March 10, 1855, was to gaze at herself in her handheld mirror and wonder why thirteen felt so much like twelve and why she saw her same self staring back at her. Diana and Elizabeth were still snuggled under the quilt. A bright ribbon of sunlight pushed through the sliver of space in the center of the shutter where the two sides didn't quite meet.

She washed herself and dressed quietly. She needed a few minutes alone with Mama and Papa. She heard the door slam and then the whack of the ax. It sounded like Moosa chopping firewood; his rhythm was faster than Papa's. As she ran down the stairs, she heard Papa and Mama talking softly in the kitchen. The room smelled of coffee—Papa's weekend treat.

Papa smiled broadly, his eyes gentle. "There's my birthday girl," he said.

Mama's lively eyes sparkled. "Happy thirteenth birthday, my sweet."

"Thank you," Maria said, sitting down at the table with them. She chose her next words carefully, as though she were measuring each one. "Mama, Papa, I'm sorry for cuffing Byron. I'll never, ever do such a thing again."

Mama picked up her cup. "Yes, my sweet. We know you're sorry."

"Did you apologize to that poor boy?" Papa asked. Maria thought that she heard a chuckle behind his question.

"Yes, Papa, and he accepted my apology. That's why I hope you'll forgive me and let me go to the meeting tonight." She stared at Papa, but addressed them both: "Mama, Papa, please, can I go for my birthday?"

Mama's eyes stopped sparkling as she took a long sip of tea. "I'm not changing my mind, Maria. You have to learn. Just saying 'I'm sorry' isn't enough."

Papa took her hand. "Maria, I know it's your birthday, but you have to learn how to hold your temper and act like a young lady." Then he kissed her on the cheek and said, "Happy birthday, daughter."

Mama stood up and walked over to the stove. "Maria, as I told you yesterday, these meetings are a serious business—not entertainment."

"I am serious. I know the meetings are not for

entertainment. But I was thinking. Maybe that lady will be there. Miss Truth. Do you think she will, Papa?"

"Perhaps. She speaks at churches and antislavery meetings," Papa said.

Mama stood up. "But you're still not going, and as I said, I don't believe you're so interested in what the lady has to say."

"But I believe in what she told us," Maria objected. "That we all must fight to end slavery."

Her father held up his hand to silence her. "Your mother is right, Maria. Now, don't pester."

They still think I'm a child, Maria thought.

Maria was sure she saw a twinkle in Papa's eyes as he took a sip of coffee. "My dear Maria," he said. "Save that cuffing for the next slave master you run into."

This would not be the birthday she wanted, and tomorrow would be worse. Miss James was sure to tell Mama about the shirt. Perhaps she should tell her parents herself, but the words were locked inside her. For a moment, the only sounds were Moosa chopping wood and Diana and Elizabeth stirring around upstairs. Instead of confessing she said, "I'll get the water this morning."

"Good. Then we'll have breakfast. I'm making your favorite, pancakes."

She hugged her mother. "Thank you, Mama."

She put on her cloak and stepped outside. Moosa had just finished chopping and rested the ax against the woodpile.

"Maria, the sun is shining just for you. Happy birthday."

"Thank you, Moosa." She picked up two of the pails near the woodpile.

Moosa picked up the other two. "I'll help you get water." He glanced at her. "Why the long face?"

"You know why. Papa and Mama said I can't go to the meeting tonight."

"I'll tell you everything," he said as they walked the few feet from their house and entered the woods. "I'll tell you in such a way you'll think you were there."

"It's not the same as being there and seeing people and hearing the speeches for myself."

"Well, perhaps they'll let you go next week."

"Not after they find out about the shirt and my examinations tomorrow."

Moosa thought for a moment and shrugged his shoulders. "Maybe Miss James won't come to church, or maybe she won't say anything to Mama and Papa. If you speak to her first, promise to make a perfect shirt."

Maria smiled for the first time that morning. "I promised Papa that I'd be perfect, and see what happened. I'll never promise to be perfect again."

Rays of sunlight streamed through the bare branches and vines, casting a soft glow. Her mood was no match for the sun that insisted on shining on her. Perhaps she could fix things.

The sunny morning and Mama's pancakes helped to lift Maria's spirits. It was, after all, *her* birthday. Moosa worked for Farmer Gruner most Saturdays, and Papa usually worked at home. There were always repairs to do on the wagon and tools to sharpen. Sometimes Papa traveled downtown to make deliveries to the stores that had put in special orders for the socks and scarves that Mama and the girls made.

Papa would be home this Saturday, and as Maria opened the store for her mother, she tossed some words around in her head trying to find just the right ones to convince him to let her go. If he said yes, Mama would relent.

After they ate breakfast, Moosa went to work, and Papa went to the stable behind the store. The happy sound of children's voices mingled with other sounds: dogs barking, wagons clanging, people hammering. Cedar Lane was wide awake on a sunny Saturday morning.

Simon pulled at Mama's skirt as she cleared the breakfast dishes. "I hear my friends. Can I go outside and play?" he asked.

"Yes, my sweet. Put on your scarf."

"Yes, Mama," he said and scrambled out of the kitchen.

Diana stopped wiping the plate she was cleaning. "Mama, can I go outside, too, when I finish?"

Mama put the plates in the tub as Elizabeth and Maria washed the cups. "No. You teased Maria, so you'll stay in and help us."

"But, Mama, this is my Saturday not to work," she whined. Except for the Saturdays when they did the wash, each girl had one Saturday off from helping in the store.

Mama put some of the scraps left from breakfast in

Dukie's plate. "Well, Maria is working, and today is her birthday."

And it's your fault, Diana, Maria thought.

"When you're done in here, I want you and Lizzie to go to the root cellar and bring up all of the onions."

Lizzie smiled sweetly. "That's a sure sign of spring." She took her hands out of the water and wiped them on her apron. "And Maria," she said, "I have a big surprise for you for your birthday."

"What is it?"

"I can't tell you; it's a surprise."

The store was always busy on Saturdays, but this Saturday seemed even busier than usual. Maria was wrapping two slices of salted fish for Sarah's mother, and Mama was helping another customer find matching buttons, when Byron's mother rushed in. Her face was twisted in such a frown that Maria was sure that she had come to complain about Maria's fight with Byron.

"Morning, ladies," she said, nodding at both Maria and Mama. "It's starting already."

Everyone stared at her, even Diana, who was still pouting as she sat at the small table and replenished the spice jars.

"What's starting?" Mama asked.

Mrs. Francis clutched her chest and breathed heavily. "My sister-in-law and her husband and two children are here on my doorstep."

Maria had just finished wrapping the salt fish and was going to talk with Papa when Reverend Arlington's sister walked in. Mama motioned for Maria to help her. So, while she measured a pound of rice flour for her, she listened to Mrs. Francis.

"They rent a house, more shack than house, on Sixtieth Street, and the owner is selling it to the city. The owner says they have to move immediately."

"Oh, my," Sarah's mother said. "What about the petition? People aren't going to try to fight this?"

The bells jangled loudly, and the Magpie flew in. "Oh, Mrs. Francis, I heard what happened to your sister-in-law. People who own property, but who don't live in it as we do, don't care about keeping it. I hear that people who rent are being thrown out of their homes like garbage thrown to the dogs." Balling her fist, she raised her arm as if leading a charge. "But we own our property, and we're going to fight this. Let them build the park around us."

Maria glanced out of the window near the door, trying not to let their talk disturb her. The sun was still shining. The Magpie was fired up. Papa had said, "Do not worry," so she wouldn't. For the first time in her life, she agreed with the Magpie. She wrapped the flour for the reverend's sister, who remained to join the conversation.

And just as she was preparing to ask her mother to excuse her for a moment, she heard Papa's wagon clanking down the road.

"Where's Papa going?"

"To the depot on Eighth Avenue. Some of his regular customers wanted him to shine their boots today."

"Is he coming back?"

"No. Moosa will meet him at the depot, and then they'll go to the meeting."

Maria wanted to stomp out of the store and walk to the meeting herself. Like Miss Truth. Walk until she got what she wanted.

The store grew busier as the day wore on, and Maria didn't have time to stew in her own juice. It seemed as if every five or ten minutes another person walked in. She measured ginger and pepper and other spices, wrapping them neatly in paper for the customers. She sliced salted fish, picked out socks and mittens, and found the right buttons and needles, and she and Diana took turns going down to the cool cellar beneath the store where carrots, potatoes, apples, lemons, buttermilk, cream, and butter were kept.

More people than usual lingered in the store through-out the day. Mama gave each customer her time and attention, listening to their talk, which was all about the city building a park where they lived.

And then the sun went down, and the store was empty. Mama let Diana go back into the house. Maria heard what sounded like small pebbles hitting the window. She looked out of the window near the door. "It was so sunny this morning, and now it's sleeting."

"That's how March is. Sunny one moment, and stormy the next." Mama smiled. "A little bit like you."

Maria chuckled and then had another thought.

Sometimes bad weather kept Miss James from going to church.

Mama looked out of the window as she folded the socks in one of the display drawers. "But you know I don't like Papa and Moosa out in this weather. See, it's a good thing I didn't let you go. I'd be worrying about all three of you."

Maria sighed as she heard the clock strike seven. She repeated Moosa's words: "You worry too much, Mama."

As soon as she walked into the house, she shouted, "I smell it. My favorite dish."

She ran over to the stove, playfully licking her lips and rubbing her stomach. Elizabeth placed a platter of salted fish mashed with potatoes, with beets and onions on the side, on the table. Elizabeth had also made a delicious plum pudding for desert. "Happy birthday, sister," she beamed.

Maria hugged Lizzie, and Dukie ran to the front door, his tail wagging like crazy.

Papa and Moosa walked in, and immediately, the house came alive, as Simon and Diana ran over to Papa. Mama finished setting the table, and Maria put more logs on the fire.

Once they all sat down at the table, Papa said a special grace for Maria. "Dear Lord, watch over and protect my eldest daughter as she steps into womanhood. Keep her safe from the temptations and tribulations of a wicked world. Keep her strong in the faith. Keep her body in good health. Amen." He said a special prayer for all of his children on their birthdays. Mama would always say, "Your papa's prayer is the best gift you could receive."

After they ate and cleaned the kitchen, they relaxed together in the sitting room. Diana gave her the sampler she'd made in school—a house surrounded by trees. Above, in meticulously stitched letters, it read, HOME IS WITH OUR FAMILY, and then underneath, FOR MY SISTER, MARIA. I LOVE YOU. Leaning over Elizabeth, Maria kissed Diana.

"This is beautiful, Diana." Maria almost forgave her.

Moosa gave her a pair of ruby-colored beaded earrings he'd purchased in one of the stores downtown. Simon sang her a song for her birthday. "This is not a bad song like the poem I said that got you and Diana in trouble," he announced.

He grinned proudly as he sang one of their Sunday school hymns, which he'd memorized just for Maria.

Simon made as deep a bow as any actor onstage, and Maria was touched. *Nothing could be better*, she thought, *than to be with my family*, even though missing the meeting still nagged at her.

Finally, Maria asked, "How was the meeting?" She looked at Moosa, waiting for his promised You Were There description. He glanced away from her as if he didn't want to say anything.

Papa answered before Moosa could speak.

"It was wonderful," he said. "Sojourner Truth spoke, and her words so touched the people that enough money was raised right then and there to free a man who escaped from Maryland. His former owner wants one thousand dollars to give him his freedom."

Mama touched her chest. "My word. Such a lot of money."

"Can you imagine that? She was able to inspire people to raise all of that money!" Papa said.

Maria saw in her mind's eye Miss Truth standing tall, her head thrown back, her voice touching every heart. "Will she be there next week?" Maria asked.

"I hope so," Papa said. "Who could sit idly by and not give a dollar or two for freedom after hearing her speak?"

"But doesn't she go to many different places?" Mama asked.

"Yes," Papa said. "She's a tireless worker. I don't know how long she'll be with us before she moves on."

Maria smiled and tried not to show how disappointed she was. "Will she come back to our church? Perhaps she'll be there tomorrow."

"I don't know," Papa said.

She'd probably never see Miss Truth again. If Miss James told her mother about the shirt, she wouldn't be going anywhere for a long time.

CHAPTER 18

THIRTEEN

THE TREES AND the roofs of the small houses glistened after the sleet and rain the night before. The Peters children held on to one another as they stepped carefully on the icy ground. Diana and Simon, though, broke away from Maria and Elizabeth and pretended to ice-skate. Dukie scampered between the two of them.

"You'll fall down and break your crown," Maria joked, but they managed to keep each other off the ground. The boulders and rocks in the distance also glistened in the morning light. The houses and buildings beyond were still hidden in the morning mist.

Maria linked arms with Elizabeth. "Lizzie, I'm wondering whether I should've told Mama about the shirt and failing my exam before we left the house this morning."

"I told you to tell her on Friday. You never take my advice."

"Maybe Miss James will be absent," Maria said. "Sometimes she doesn't come to church when it's snowy or icy and the railroad cars hardly run, especially the colored cars."

"Miss James doesn't have to ride the colored cars."

"How do you know that, Lizzie?"

"I heard Mama say so. She said that the conductors don't always realize that Miss James is a colored lady, so she can ride any car that comes along. She still might come to church."

"I'll talk to her before she gets a chance to speak to Mama or Papa. Since she's the superintendent of the Sunday school, she's there early, before Mama and Papa come to church. So why rile Mama up for no reason?"

"What will you tell Miss James?"

"I won't tell her anything. I'll beg. I'll get on my knees if I have to and beg her not to tell Mama. I'll promise to do two more shirts and even a plain dress."

Elizabeth stopped walking. "You? A dress?"

"I could do it if I put my mind to it. And I'll help Anna, too. I'll help her so well she'll be writing her name by the end of next week."

They walked past Sarah's house on one side of the road and the Magpie's on the other. There was no sign of Sarah, and Maria remembered that this was the Sunday she had intended to ask Mama and Papa about not attending Sunday school with the younger children. She now thought better of it.

As they neared the church, a sloppy snowball whizzed past their heads. They ducked and saw Byron slipping and sliding toward the church and the school buildings. "You and Byron are friends again, Maria?"

"Yes," she said, looking around for real snow among the icy mess on the side of the path. "He can't help it if he's a silly boy."

She couldn't find enough snow to make a solid snowball, so she raised her fist and grinned. "I'll get you for that, Byron."

"Not if I get you first," Byron said as he ran around to the side of the church before Maria could reach him.

Maria braced herself as she neared the church. She looked around for Miss James among the people milling about in the small entranceway. Miss James wasn't there; otherwise she'd have been talking with Mrs. Ball.

Maria looked inside the sanctuary. Some people were already sitting in pews, but she didn't see Miss James among them. Maria was relieved. "See, Miss James isn't here," she said to Elizabeth.

"She might come later," Elizabeth said.

"I doubt it." Maria looked around. "I wonder whether Anna and her parents will come today. I hope so." *And maybe Miss Truth will come, too,* she thought.

As Miss Ball started leading the children down the steps to the basement, Byron and several other boys rushed in.

"Okay, children," said Mrs. Ball. "It's time for Sunday school. Get in size places. Come, now."

Maria walked down the steps to the church basement. She peeped at Simon, making sure he wasn't pushing and shoving.

Mrs. Ball tried to make the younger ones settle down. Some Sundays there were very few younger children, but today there were more than usual. Maria sat next to Sarah, who had arrived earlier, and Byron sat behind them. Mrs. Ball motioned for Maria and Byron to come to the front of the room. "Byron, I want you to do the readings, and Sarah and Maria, I want you to sit with the little ones and make sure they pay attention as I give the lesson. And help them sing the hymn."

Sunday school passed quickly for Maria, probably because of helping Mrs. Ball with the younger students. She felt like a monitor—a Sunday school monitor.

When Sunday school ended, Maria rushed out of the basement and upstairs to see whether Miss James was in church; once again, she was relieved. Miss James was nowhere in sight. Maria was happy, though, to see Anna with her parents.

Anna's mother was very thin and very tall. She wore the same cloak Anna had been wearing to school, and Maria could see why it had looked so big and long on Anna. This Sunday, Anna wore a gray cloak that fit properly. Her father was a little shorter than her mother, and very muscular and stocky. Anna's mother looked nervous and uncomfortable; her father held his head high and his back straight. They were talking to the two women from the Dorcas Society, the church benevolent organization that helped poor people. Maria thought that maybe Anna had gotten her cloak from the ladies in the society.

Maria looked around for her parents and Moosa, anxious to introduce them to Anna's family. Soon she found them.

"Papa, my friend Anna, from school, is here," she said.

Mama frowned. "What girl? The one who told you that horrible story?"

Just as Maria turned around to point Anna out, Miss James loomed over her like a cloud. Maria's heart raced, and she actually began to sweat. She had been certain that Miss James was absent. Mama held Simon's hand; Diana and Elizabeth walked over to them.

Maria couldn't look at Lizzie, but her sister's words rolled around in her head: *You never take my advice.*

"Mr. and Mrs. Peters," Miss James began, "I am so happy to see you."

Maria stared at the floor just as Anna always did.

"Elizabeth and Diana will be promoted. They have both done very well. Diana has calmed down considerably, and Elizabeth is an excellent student." She paused, and it seemed to Maria that every eye was on them and that every ear was straining to hear what Miss James had to say next. "I am sorry to report," Miss James continued, "that Maria did not pass all of her examinations."

Maria did not dare look into Miss James's eyes. She kept her head lowered, staring at the wooden floor.

"What's this?" Mama asked.

Maria felt her father's stare burning the top of her bowed head.

"But she's a smart girl," Papa said. "Maria, how could you fail your examinations?"

"I'm sorry, Papa," she mumbled.

"She failed sewing," Miss James said.

Both Mama and Papa said at the same time: "Sewing?"

"How could you cipher and read the way you do and fail such an easy thing as sewing?" Papa asked. "Explain that to me."

"She can do the work, she just doesn't want to. She let another student finish her shirt. Someone else did her work. A new girl, who didn't know better."

She looked at her mother, and tried to force out a tear, but she was too angry to cry. This was too much fuss over a shirt. "I didn't know she was going to make the whole shirt for me," she mumbled.

Mama's small face was pinched. "Maria, what is wrong with you? The fighting, now this?"

Maria bowed her head as low as she could without snapping her neck. "I'm sorry, Mama."

She could feel Papa's angry gaze as he spoke. "Miss James, she'll do better. Failing something as simple as sewing. And you cheated," he added, now directing his words at his daughter.

"Miss James, this will not happen again. She will do everything she has to do," Mama said. She, too, turned back to Maria. "I've asked you time and time again how you were doing, and you lied and told me you were doing better. And you let that student do your work. I could've helped you; Lizzie could have helped; you know she's first-rate; even Diana could have helped you."

Maria didn't have to look. She knew Diana was grinning from ear to ear. Simon whispered loudly to Elizabeth, "Is Maria in trouble?"

Mama turned to them. "You children, go and play until it's time for church."

Maria kept her head low as she tried mightily not to cry. "I'm sorry, Mama," she mumbled. "I really didn't mean to cheat or lie."

Papa started to speak, but a soft female voice stopped him. "Sir, missus, can I talk with you for a moment if it please you?"

Mama stared in surprise at the tall, thin woman standing before her. "Your daughter been so nice to my Anna. We just come here, and your Maria is the only friend she have." Anna stood shyly behind her parents.

"Oh, thank you—I'm happy to know that." Mama appeared to have trouble, at first, understanding Anna's mother. "Is your daughter the new girl, who finished Maria's sewing?"

"Yes, ma'am. Because Maria been showing her the ABCs. She tell me about Maria. That's all she talk about— her friend, Maria, and how Maria have so much trouble with a needle and thread, and she just want to help her."

Both sets of parents walked toward the sanctuary together, and Maria felt a little relieved. Whatever punishment she received would perhaps be tempered by Anna's mother's good words. Moosa walked over to Maria and put his arm around her shoulder. "Come on, Maria. Don't feel bad. They won't stay angry with you forever."

She wiped her eyes with the back of her hand. "One day everyone is so proud of me, and the next day I'm in trouble."

"They'll forgive you," Moosa said. And then he said, "Hello."

Maria looked up and saw Anna standing in front of her.

Anna seemed shyer than usual, so Maria introduced her to Moosa, who then excused himself and went to talk with several other young men.

"Your mother saved me," Maria said.

"She just saying what's true. We was coming to say hello, and I tell my ma that you were my friend. I know Miz James was saying about the shirt, so I figure you need a good word from somewhere. I knew my mother would say something nice about you."

Church hadn't started yet, so the two girls linked arms and stepped outside. Anna looked up at the sun and smiled. "I'm glad it's getting warmer. I'm not used to this cold," she said, and then abruptly stopped, as if she wanted to take the words back. "I mean, I don't like such cold weather. It gets inside your bones."

Maria looked directly at her, and Anna seemed to

avoid her eyes. "It's no colder than it always is in New York," Maria said.

"I know, but you never get used to it." Anna was suddenly quiet, as if she'd said something wrong. Then she changed the subject. "What did you do yesterday for your birthday? My mother take in laundry, and I had to help her all day."

Maria showed her the ruby red earrings Moosa had given her and told her about how she had celebrated.

The sun was fighting its way through the clouds. The ground was wet now with small streams of water trickling around them and puddles settling on the road.

"Anna, you'll come every Sunday? Come to Sunday school and we can sit together." Maria knew that she'd be going to Sunday school for a while longer.

"I'll ask my mama. I think she'll say yes."

Church began, and Anna sat with her parents in one of the back pews; they appeared lonely and out of place. Maria turned around a few times, wondering whether Miss Truth would be there again. Every time she turned around, though, she seemed to look straight into the Magpie's eyes. She slid down in her seat. If only Miss Truth were there to sing and preach again and lift her spirits. But she was nowhere to be seen.

CHAPTER 19

SWEET HOME

WHEN THEY LEFT the church, Simon and Diana zigzagged more than they walked, looking completely refreshed after their long nap in church. Dukie, who had been waiting for them outside, followed. Papa walked along with Mr. and Mrs. Davis, and Little Miss waved to Maria and went into her house. Then Papa stopped to chat with Mr. Davis for a moment. Probably talking about the property, Maria thought.

Mama smiled and nodded as the Magpie's mouth moved incessantly. Even when they reached her house, she kept talking to Mama. Maria walked on by herself.

She wondered what Mama and Papa would say to her once they were home. She was still only a new thirteen, and a spanking was a real possibility.

* * *

When they reached home, all Mama said was, "Girls, change your clothing. We'll bake bannock for supper."

Diana ran upstairs. "That's my favorite," she said. Elizabeth raced behind her. Maria escaped to the privy, the one place where she could have total privacy. She didn't want Elizabeth and Diana asking her questions about what Mama and Papa had said to her in church. When she guessed that they'd finished changing into their everyday dresses, she went upstairs and changed, too.

Back downstairs, Diana was reading Bible stories to Simon from a children's book Papa had brought home. Moosa was stretched out on the floor before the fireplace, fast asleep.

"Oh, here she is," Mama said. "Maria, sift the meal." She handed Elizabeth the jar of molasses. "Only add two spoonfuls, Lizzie."

The bannock, or Indian cake, as some people called it, would go along with the leftover salted fish and potatoes from Maria's birthday supper the night before. Mama insisted on keeping the Sabbath as much as possible, and so Sunday was the time to rest. When they didn't eat at Grandma Isabella's, their Sunday meal was always leftovers from Saturday night or prepared on Saturday.

"Don't forget to put in two teaspoonfuls of salt," Mama reminded Maria. Mama's small face appeared pinched and stern. Maria would much rather have seen her mother with one hand on her hip and the other wagging a finger in her face, chastising her. She wished her mother would say something, anything; tell her what her punishment would be.

Papa usually visited with Byron's father on Sundays, or sat in the rocker and slept, or asked Maria or Lizzie to read the paper to him. This Sunday, he was fixing the wheel on the wagon and banging harder than seemed necessary. Maria wondered if he were so angry with her that he was making believe the wheel was her head. When he stopped banging the wheel, he started chopping wood, which she and Moosa always did on Mondays, never on Sundays.

Mama added a small lump of shortening. "Keep stirring," she said. "Lizzie, make sure the pan is hot, and Maria, grease it well. Girls, make sure you smooth out the batter and brown it well on both sides." She fussed and hovered over them. "Take the lard back to the cellar as soon as you finish using it. I don't want it to melt."

"We can do the rest, Mama," Maria said.

"Okay. I'll be outside with your father."

Elizabeth immediately whispered to Maria. "What's wrong with Mama? What did she say to you in church? Are you punished yet?"

"No, she didn't punish me yet, and she's probably outside now talking to Papa about what my punishment should be." Maria sliced a piece of lard and rubbed the inside of the baking pan with it.

"Why do you think they're talking about you?"

"They seem angry."

"What makes you think you're so important?" Elizabeth asked. "Do you think Mama will spank you?"

She sighed, "Don't ask me that. I'm thirteen now. I'm too old to be spanked."

"Does Mama think so?"

Maria didn't answer her. "I'm going to take the lard back to the cellar."

She walked down the narrow hallway that led to the store and pulled up the door that was built into the floor. She climbed down the stairs and into the cold cellar with its bright, whitewashed walls. A tiny window let in light. Shelves carved into the wall held carrots, beets, and apples. Mama stored potatoes and heads of cabbage for the winter in holes dug into the ground below the shelves.

Maria opened a large wooden closet with wire sides and replaced the lard. She rearranged the cream, butter, eggs, and cheese, just to have another moment alone.

Elizabeth was putting the batter in the pan when Maria went back upstairs.

"Well, I don't think you need my help, do you?" Maria asked.

"No. I can brown the cakes."

Maria walked over to Moosa. He snored loudly. She nudged him gently and sprawled next to him.

"Moosa, what's wrong with Mama and Papa? Mama won't speak to me, and Papa is outside working, and they're talking. Maybe they're thinking of a way to punish me."

"You know Papa's going to City Hall tomorrow. I think he's worried about the petition. Whether we will have to move." Moosa hesitated a moment. "I think Papa would move to Kansas if we had to leave New York." He was silent for a moment, as if in deep thought. "But you know what I think. He should take the money for this property and head straight to California."

Maria listened to Diana's lilting voice as she read to Simon. The clock ticked, and she gazed at the large sofa and Mama's colorful quilt thrown over the back. This was her sweet home. "I don't want to live anywhere else but here, Moosa. You know that."

He lifted Maria's chin. "Don't fret over it, Maria. Anything could happen. Papa will stare down the mayor and the city council and everyone else at City Hall, and they will change their minds." He threw his head back and laughed loudly. "They will build a park around us."

She felt better. "The Magpie said the same thing."

Maria tried to read Mama's and Papa's faces as they all sat down to a silent supper. Why wouldn't they speak to her?

When they had almost finished eating, Papa finally spoke. "You know, tomorrow we're taking the petition to the City Hall."

"What's a petition?" Diana asked.

Papa patiently continued. "We don't know how successful we'll be. Only time will tell. But I don't want you children to be frightened." He looked at Mama and then at the girls. "I know you'll hear talk in school about people thrown out on the streets and such. Don't believe them. Remember, home is with our family."

Maria looked over at Moosa, who kept eating. Was he listening to Papa? she wondered. She gazed at her family again and understood what Papa was really saying. When they were together, no matter where they were, they were home.

After they finished eating, Maria and Elizabeth washed the dishes in the tub and dried them. As she swept the floor, Maria waited for her punishment, but Diana was the only one talking. "Can we move downtown to Grandma's house? I like it down there. Maria, where do you want to move to?"

Maria didn't offer an answer, and Diana didn't wait for one. "I like it at Grandma's; then I can see the people dance."

"Those are not nice people," Mama reminded her. "Dancing on the Lord's Day like that. And no one said we're moving."

When the clock struck ten, Mama began to put out the lamps, and everyone headed off to bed. Just as Maria was getting ready to follow Elizabeth up the stairs, Mama called out to her: "Maria, come here a moment."

Now it's coming, Maria thought.

"Maria, I know you could have done the sewing if you tried. I want you to be promoted in all of your subjects."

"Yes, Mama." She hung her head and clasped her hands behind her back.

"I like the way you helped the girl in your class, and I can understand if you have trouble sewing. Not all women are gifted in that area." She spread her arms as though she were frustrated. "You didn't try. That's what makes me

angry, Maria. And that's what makes a person a failure—
when she doesn't try. I know you can do plain, basic needlework. And the cheating is the worst thing."

"But, Mama, I didn't mean to cheat." Maria leaned in
toward her mother, pleading with her eyes. "I didn't mean
for Anna to sew the whole shirt."

"You cheated when you let her take the shirt home.
You know that's against the rules."

"Mama, I'm sorry. I'll make another shirt and I'll even
try to make a plain dress. I'll do . . ."

Mama held up her hand and stopped her. "That's
enough. I don't want all of these promises. But you will
finish that shirt, so that you can be promoted to the Class
of Merit and be a monitor."

It was so quiet upstairs Maria was sure that Elizabeth
and Diana were standing outside the door to their bedroom, listening. "Yes, Mama," she said and searched deep
in her heart for Miss Truth's determination. "Mama, if I
finish the shirt this week, can I go to the meeting with
Papa and Moosa next Saturday?"

Mama put her hands on her hips. "No. You will stay
home with us. I have to see you act a lot more responsibly.
Go upstairs and make sure you say your prayers."

"Yes, Mama," Maria said, and she walked up the stairs.
Thirteen, and nothing had changed. So Maria thought.

CHAPTER 20

LOYAL FRIEND

ARIA HAD A restless sleep. Thoughts about what would happen next, whether they would have to move, and shame over the shirt gave her no peace. When she finally lurched into sleep, the morning seemed to come too quickly, and she was worn out.

This Monday was so different from the usual Monday morning routine that she thought the whole day would move sideways instead of forward, if such a thing were possible.

It was strange to see Papa leaving the house before they'd finished breakfast, dressed in the frock coat he wore on Sundays, and it was stranger still to see Farmer Gruner coming by in his horse and wagon to pick him up so that they could ride downtown to City Hall.

Moosa drove their own horse and wagon downtown

in order to deliver Mama's buttermilk for Papa. Next he would go to the railroad depots to shine shoes, so that Papa's regular customers could go home with clean boots. Maria saw the worried look in Mama's eyes as she kissed them good-bye, even as she said cheerily, "Be good today, my sweets."

When they reached the school yard, Maria sensed the same ominous strangeness that she'd felt at home; perhaps it was because it was so out of place not to see Miss James standing in front of the girls' building this sunny morning. The girls and boys ran and hit each other and fell and wrestled as if they'd all gone mad. She saw Anna standing near the front of the building with a new little ABCer by her side. When Anna saw Maria, she walked toward her. The new student followed Anna, who took her hand.

"She think I her teacher or something," Anna laughed. Then she whispered, "Nothing I can teach her 'cept ABC."

"That's more than she already knows. I hope Miss James lets me help you again. I could get you to *H* by Friday."

"I hear one of the girls saying the school is closing tomorrow, and that's why Miss James ain't here today. That's not true, is it? She just went to the City Hall, isn't that so?"

Maria nodded. "That's right. She'll be back tomorrow."

Large white clouds tumbled across the sky as the sun fought to shine. Headmaster Clark stepped out of the boys' building and had to shout to get the boys to line up properly. Maria had never heard him raise his voice like that. Little Miss glided out of the girls' building holding her head very high and tilting it slightly to the right, just as Miss James did.

She didn't wear a plain dress and apron like everyone else, but a taffeta dress with a hoop underneath and ruffles down the front. Since she was the head monitor, she would be substituting for Miss James. Another item to add to the list of strange developments that day.

Sarah joined the girls and pointed to Little Miss. "Isn't she grand?" They all giggled.

Headmaster Clark approached Little Miss, and Maria guessed that he was giving her instructions for the day. Naomi and the other monitors tried to get the girls to settle down as they walked into the building. The youngest girls were quiet, paying attention to the monitors' instructions to line up silently.

The girls in the third form, Diana's group, kept talking. Diana's mouth moved so fast Maria thought it would slide off her face and clack across the ground on its own. Even some of the girls in Elizabeth's form ignored the monitors' instructions to stop talking. Elizabeth put her fingers to her lips, trying to help settle her classmates down. They ignored her, too.

When they reached the classroom, some of the girls pushed and shoved their way to the closet. Little Miss still tried to pose like Miss James at the podium. "Girls, you'd better behave," she said, "or I will have all of you punished."

They ignored her. Two students from the fourth

form, who still wore their fancy pantalets from Examination Day, dramatically clutched their hearts as though they were fainting when they saw Miss James's empty desk. "We miss her so much," one of them exclaimed.

"How can we have school without her?" the other one called out, staring at Little Miss, who picked up Miss James's Bible. "Girls, girls, stop it! Stop talking!" she yelled. "We are still having school, even though Miss James isn't here." She clapped her hands the way Miss James usually did.

Maria turned to Sarah. "These girls have lost their minds."

"The monitors are supposed to know how to make them behave," Sarah said. "I wish they'd stop acting the fool so we could get started."

Maria gazed around the room. "If I were a monitor, I could make them behave."

A girl in the third form raised a thin little hand. She didn't live on Cedar Lane, but farther down the hill. "I don't want the school to close tomorrow."

Her comment set off another round of talking and commotion. Diana cried, "Is school closed tomorrow?"

Maria knew that she would never have done that if Miss James had been there. She stood up at her desk and called across the room to Diana. "You're repeating gossip. Now, be quiet, so we can begin the day."

Diana rolled her eyes at her, but was quiet.

Several of the monitors began to talk to each other, not even paying attention to the students. The little ones seemed to sense the growing revolt, and they began to chatter. The only ABC student who was quiet was the little girl whom Anna had befriended. Maria smiled to herself. Anna had her slate and chalk and was showing the child how to form a letter.

Suddenly, Maria turned to Sarah. "I know how to stop this."

"How?"

"Watch me." Maria picked up her composition book and her pen, boldly stomped up to the front, and sat at Miss James's desk. She dipped her pen in the inkwell and began to write.

"What is Maria doing sitting there at Miss James's desk? Why don't you make her leave?" a girl asked, pointing toward Maria.

Little Miss turned around and frowned. "What are you doing?" she asked Maria.

Maria stood up. "I'm writing down the names of all of these rude girls," she said firmly. She stared at Amy, who was wearing frilly bloomers. "When your mother comes to my mother's store, I'm going to tell her everything you've done."

"Oh, no, Maria!"

Maria ignored her and called the name of another girl. "Emily. Your mother comes into the store every evening. I'm going to tell her how you were so rude that we couldn't start school."

"I'm not rude, Maria. You'd better not tell my mother any such thing," Emily said.

"Then you'd better sit down."

Emily sat down, and Diana looked at Maria with wide, surprised eyes. Elizabeth smiled slightly. Suddenly all was quiet. The monitors stood in front of their forms.

Maria nodded at Little Miss. "They're quiet now," she said. "You can proceed." She couldn't believe how much she sounded like Miss James. She giggled to herself as she sat back down at Miss James's desk.

Little Miss, looking annoyed, mumbled, "Thank you." She started the Bible reading.

A group of girls in the second form began to wiggle in their seats. When Little Miss finished, Maria stood up and stared at them. "I know your mothers, too. Do you want me to give them a bad report when I see them in church?"

They immediately quieted down. The girls in the Class of Merit put their compositions on Miss James's desk. Maria picked them up and handed them to Elizabeth. "Put these safely in Miss James's office." Elizabeth followed her orders.

"Miss James didn't tell you to be in charge," one of the girls in the pantalets said, standing up and facing Maria.

"And she didn't tell you to be in charge, either, running your mouth and not listening to the monitors. I'll tell her that."

The girl sat back down in a huff. The reading monitor wrote the assignment for the day for each group on the lesson charts hanging from the wall.

Then the writing monitor walked from group to group

and dictated the twelve words that each reading group must write on their slates. Meanwhile, Anna practiced the letters she'd learned. Maria was pleased that, at least for the moment, Anna was also writing on her slate and seemed to be doing the same thing as everyone else.

After the dictation was checked, the girls had to work out their addition, subtraction, multiplication, and division exercises. Maria helped the arithmetic monitor with the girls in the second form, who were doing single-digit multiplication.

She then stood before the girls in the sixth form and helped them work out all of their division problems. In the meantime, she hadn't done her own work; but she couldn't stop herself. She even sat down in the front with Anna and showed her how to form the letters *E* and *F*.

"This is easy," Anna said. "Just straight lines."

A half hour before lunch recess, Maria began to work on her long-division problems. Everything was back to normal, as if Miss James were sitting behind her desk.

Headmaster Clark walked into the room. "Monitors," he exclaimed, "you are doing a wonderful job." He bounded to the front of the room, his hands clasped together.

"Monitors, I am so proud of the mature way in which you are conducting yourselves. Miss James will be proud, also, when I tell her how well you've ordered the school."

He looked at the rest of the girls. "I'm so happy to see the way you girls are listening to your monitors." He nodded toward Little Miss. "You are handling this very well, Miss Davis. I will be talking to your parents. Keep up the good work."

He started walking down the incline when, suddenly, Anna raised her hand. "Suh! Suh!" she called out. "Please, can I speak with you?"

He turned around obviously surprised and a little irritated that Anna had stopped him. "Yes?"

"Uh, suh, it was Maria who make them behave." She turned around and pointed at Maria.

Maria wanted to slide under her desk. "Oh, why did she say that?" she whispered to Sarah, who murmured, "Well, it's true, but still, I'm surprised she had the nerve to say anything."

Little Miss said to the headmaster, "The girls were upset because Miss James wasn't here. Maria helped to settle them down."

Naomi added, "She was a very good help, Headmaster Clark."

Anna returned to writing *E*'s and *F*'s on her slate as if she hadn't said a word.

"Well, that's wonderful, Maria. I will tell Miss James about you, too," he said.

Finally. Finally, someone will report something good about me, thought Maria. "Thank you, Headmaster Clark," she said.

As the headmaster left, the church bells chimed twelve times. The sun shone so brightly that most of the girls ate their lunch outside. Little Miss approached Maria as she took her dinner basket out of the closet. "I was going to tell him, Maria. I just didn't get a chance to before Anna opened her mouth."

Maria smiled sweetly. "It doesn't matter."

And it really didn't matter to Maria. Anna was all that mattered—she was a good and loyal friend.

CHAPTER 21

ANNA'S REAL STORY

ONLY ANNA, MARIA, and several monitors ate inside the classroom. Sunshine brightened the room, adding a bit of luster even to the slates that hung from the sides of the desks.

"Anna, thank you for saying nice things about me."

"I had to. Them girls was taking the credit for all what you did."

She realized that Anna was not as shy as she seemed, and that maybe she hung her head for a different reason. Maria opened her dinner basket. She took out the Indian cake from the night before and offered Anna a slice of bread and cheese.

"No, ma'am," Anna said. "I have my own lunch today. You like some corn bread?"

"No, ma'am," Maria smiled. "I don't want to eat up

all of your lunch." But she thought that the corn bread smelled extra good.

Anna took a bite. "I think I get you in trouble. But my ma say you seem like a nice girl, and she glad we is friends. So, you think Miz James let us help each other like before?"

"She might let me help you after I finish the shirt."

"It seem like a silly thing to put you in trouble just because you slow with the needle."

Maria liked Anna's funny way of expressing herself. "'Slow with the needle' isn't as bad as 'dimwit,' is it?"

"A dimwit is a mighty stupid fella. You not stupid," Anna said.

Maria took an apple out of her basket. She could hear the cries of a flock of gulls mingling with the laughter and shouts of her schoolmates outside.

Anna moved close to Maria. "Ma'am, do you really think the city will build a park here and we have to leave? That's what the girls keep saying."

"They say they will, but that's why my father and Miss James and some other people signed a petition to get the city to change its plans."

"I don't want to leave here," said Anna. Suddenly she looked around as if she were seeing everything for the first time. "I love the school and living here. I don't want to move."

"I don't, either," Maria said. She stared at Anna's scarred hands. "But you have your parents. That's what my papa told us—not to worry as long as we're together."

"I hear my mother and father talking. We moving, too,

and I don't want to move again. I get used to here. I like it. We always moving. All the time."

"Moving all the time?" Maria asked. "When did you move before? I thought you came from downtown."

Anna lowered her head and put her hand over her eyes.

"Anna, Anna, what's wrong? Are you crying?"

Anna wiped her eyes and leaned closer to Maria, her voice lower than a whisper. "Ma'am, I have something to tell you, but you have to promise not to say anything to no one. My parents kill me if they know I tell. You have to promise."

"I promise."

"We was slaves." The words, whispered so softly, floated around Maria's ears, but didn't really get inside her head. It was as if everything stopped—the girls talking quietly, the sounds of the children outside laughing, yelling, squealing, giggling. Silence.

"You hear me, Maria? We was slaves."

Maria knew about slavery. It was discussed in church, at school, and at home. Moosa and Papa had seen and heard the great Frederick Douglass, who had been a slave, speak at an antislavery meeting, and they had talked about it over and over. And she had seen and heard Miss Truth. But Anna was a girl, like herself. A nice girl, who knew how to tell stories and sew perfect shirts. A normal girl. A friend.

"You're free now?" Maria asked in a hoarse whisper.

"My father says we are. He always say we free our own selves," she whispered softly. Maria could hardly hear her. "Don't tell anyone, you promise?"

Maria nodded, and Anna told her story, simply and plainly.

"My parents buy their freedom from the woman who own us. She used to rent my father and mother out to do work for other people. She keep the money they make and give a little of it to them. They save every penny."

She lowered her head again, and finally Maria understood why. She was showing too much of herself.

"Where were you when your parents worked?"

"I was always with the cook. I help her in the kitchen every day. My mother work nearby and come home every night. We live in a cabin in the quarters. My father come to visit us once in a while because he work on a farm far away.

"I help the cook shell peas, cut up food, I pick greens for her. She teach me how to cook. Then when I a little older one of the slave women who do the spinning teach me how to sew and spin, and I begin to work with the women in the spinning house. I take to the sewing and spinning real good.

"My mother keep me close to her side as much as she could. I always work, but we have fun at Christmastime. We go from cabin to cabin bringing food. People singing and dancing. We have church out in the fields.

"Finally, both my parents pay for their freedom, but the woman who own us say that I was a apprentice. That she fed and clothed me and raise me and taught me, so legally, she say, I still belong to her, 'til I'm eighteen." Anna looked angry.

"The woman say if my parents want me they have to pay her five hundred dollars. Otherwise, I stay with her." Anna wiped her eyes, and Maria fought to keep her own tears back.

"Don't cry yet," Anna said. "You ain't hear the worse of the story. My parents don't have the money, but my father ain't listen to her. One night he come to the cabin and we take off.

"A man my father met help us escape. We go to different places. I don't know where. We stay in a swamp. We ride on a rowboat. We be in different cabin with different people. And all the time my father tell us we is free, but we have to keep moving. He say, one human can't own another. Then, when we come here, my father say, 'No more running. New York is a free state.'

"The man who help us escape even find a place for us to stay. It was nasty, though. On Baxter Street, where I told you we was from. But Maria, that fella was a scoundrel. My father had to pay him for his help, and once he settle us in he go back to Virginia and tell the woman exactly where we are. So he could get more money for turning us in. That's why we leave from downtown."

Maria leaned closer to Anna. "What? I don't understand."

"People get money for turning in runaways. No sooner we get to New York than the lawman comes after my father saying that he owes the woman five hundred dollars for me, and that my mother and father could be arrested for stealing me."

Maria thought about the stories they'd often read in the papers, about people who were accused of being fugitives and sent back to slavery. "Oh, Anna, that's terrible. What're your parents going to do?"

"My mother say we need to leave New York and try to get to Canada, then nobody come after me."

Now Maria understood. "Someone is after you? Is that why your mother always meets you?"

Anna nodded. "My mother tell me that since we only rent the shack we live in, we have to leave soon, because the owner is selling his property to the city."

"Maybe your parents could rent a room in one of the houses on Cedar Lane. Mrs. Hamilton, our neighbor, rents rooms. See, maybe the city won't tear down our houses and school and church, since everyone signed a petition," she said innocently, as if saying it might make it true. "I have to help you, Anna."

"There's nothing you can do."

"You're my best friend. I have to help you."

Anna looked Maria squarely in the eye. "I never had a friend before. That's the best thing you do for me."

The afternoon was calmer than the morning because the girls sewed and made dolls, and they were allowed to talk and sit with friends. Anna sat in the back with Maria, but with their classmates seated around them the two friends could not continue their conversation from lunch. Instead Maria showed Anna the letter *G* and began once again to sew her plain shirt. She began with a sleeve, hemming it on either side. And as she struggled to make every stitch straight and neat, Anna copied and recopied the letter.

"This letter ain't so easy to get."

Maria put down her sewing and placed her hand over Anna's. "Start up here, Anna. Come around to the left, then stop here and draw a short line, like so."

Sarah chattered to another girl about a boy in the boys' school who was so hateful, and other gossip. Naomi mentioned moving, and everyone agreed that they had nothing to worry about. "How can the city tear down our school and houses?" Naomi asked.

"Not to mention our church," another girl said.

Maria was quiet. Some people, she thought, might be moving right away.

When school ended for the day, Maria waved sadly to Anna and watched her walk down the hill toward the shanties and home. The tall, dark figure of her mother was visible, waiting there.

Elizabeth pulled on her arm. "Why didn't you come out and play at lunchtime? Byron asked about you," she said, glancing coyly at her sister.

"I was showing Anna her letters." Maria looked at Diana, who was walking, hopping, skipping, and dancing ahead of them.

"It was so nice out this afternoon."

Maria shrugged her shoulders as they passed an outcropping of rock just before entering Cedar Lane. "Anna and I just didn't feel like going outside."

As they walked along the road and passed Byron's house, he shouted, "I'll race you tomorrow, Maria!"

She made believe she hadn't heard him.

"There's something the matter with you, Maria."

"I was just wondering what happened at City Hall today."

No sooner had she said that than they reached the Magpie's house. Mrs. Hamilton came flying out her door. "Hello, hello, children. Your father is back. I saw him riding up the road a few minutes ago with Farmer Gruner. I'm on my way to your mother's store now."

She rushed past them before they had a chance to return her greeting. The small cap she usually wore indoors looked as though it were sliding off her head.

Maria and Elizabeth walked faster, trying to catch up with her. "I wonder what happened," Elizabeth said.

"I bet the store is already filled with people. You know how fast news travels around here," Maria said.

When they reached Mama's garden plot, Dukie came bounding out with Simon following him, yelling, "Papa's home."

Diana dashed into the store first, with Maria and Elizabeth following. The Magpie and Farmer Gruner, Reverend Arlington, and Papa were there. Mama wrapped a large piece of salted codfish for Mrs. Francis.

Papa stopped talking when the girls came in. "There's my girls." Diana ran over to him, and he kissed her. Maria saw that his eyes were calm.

Papa resumed talking, and Maria listened closely as

she hung up her cloak; Elizabeth stood quietly next to her. Diana slipped behind the counter with Mama, her eyes wide with curiosity.

"Of course we couldn't see Mayor Wood. And when Mr. O'Brien, you know, the Irish fellow who lives on the next road, asked if we could leave the petition for the mayor and aldermen, the clerk wanted to know who O'Brien had voted for in the last election."

"So, what did you say?" the Magpie asked.

"Nothing. We didn't have to," Farmer Gruner interrupted. "You women never let us get a word in." He grinned at the Magpie, who looked insulted.

Then Reverend Arlington took up the story. "The lovely schoolteacher, Mistress James, spoke up," he said. "Miss James said that she was a public-school teacher who also owned property that would be taken, and on behalf of her fellow property owners, she was presenting the petition. She then said that all of the gentlemen were property owners and voters."

"So, Solomon, what do you think will come of it all?" the Magpie asked Papa.

"I don't know. There was a crowd of people down there, too." Papa folded his arms and looked amused. "One fellow threatened to burn down the City Hall if the city took his property."

Even with all the talk around her, she couldn't help thinking of Anna at that moment. Everyone was concerned with holding on to their property, but Anna was being treated as if she herself were a piece of property.

She wished she could tell everyone in the store about it, so that they'd be angry along with her.

Later on that evening, after dinner, Maria knitted a pair of socks to make up for all of the needlework she hadn't done. Elizabeth read the papers to Papa. Moosa, who came in late after taking care of all of Papa's customers, was stretched out in front of the fireplace, snoring loudly. Poor Dukie had to take himself to the other side of the room, where he lay under the kitchen table.

Simon and Diana quietly played Rabbit on the Wall.

Maria fought the urge to wake Moosa and ask him what she should do about Anna. She wanted to help, but she couldn't break her promise. As she knit, her mother looked over at her.

"Maria, that looks good. Now, that's something your father could sell."

Mama continued to gaze at the socks and then said, "You know, Maria, when I was your age, we had a girls' sewing circle called the Sugar Plums. We raised money for the antislavery society."

Mama's words were a gift. Suddenly, Maria knew how she could help Anna.

CHAPTER 22

A WONDERFUL IDEA

"**W**HAT'S YOUR HURRY?" Elizabeth asked as Maria practically ran down Cedar Lane, not even stopping to wait for Sarah, who had just come out of her house. Diana walked along behind them with Amy and several of their classmates.

"Am I hurrying? I didn't think so. I just want to get to school. It's freezing out here."

Elizabeth stared at her sister. "It's not that cold. Why are you in such a rush?"

"I'm not," Maria said, moving even faster once they passed Little Miss's house. She hoped that Anna would be at school this morning. Anna had to be the first person to hear her idea. She couldn't even tell Elizabeth.

"Do you think Miss James will be there today?" Elizabeth asked as they passed the outcropping of rock that came just before they reached the school yard.

"Yes," Maria said. "Why wouldn't she be? She doesn't have any more petitions to turn in."

When Maria entered the school yard, it seemed as if every girl she'd chastised the day before smiled in her direction. "Hi, Maria!"; "Good morning, Maria!"; "Hello, Maria."

"Don't worry," she replied, "I'm not going to tell on you." She looked around for Anna and spotted her sitting on the bench near the front of the girls' building, next to the little ABCer who had taken such a liking to her.

As she ran toward them she noticed that there seemed to be fewer girls around than usual, but it was still early. "Anna, I have something to tell you. I have an idea."

Anna stood up and walked toward her, leaving the little girl behind on the bench. "An idea?" she asked.

"An idea to help you. If your father goes to the antislavery meeting with my father on Saturday he can tell them what happened. Last week, Miss Truth was there, and they raised enough money to free a man who'd escaped from Maryland."

Anna frowned. "I can't tell him that. He'll be angry if he thought I told anyone."

"Well, tell him that I told you about the antislavery meeting, but that it's your idea and you think he should go." She shivered and saw a few of the girls lining up. "The church is on Leonard Street."

"He knows the church. But after what the man did to us, he trust nobody."

Maria sighed. "But he knows my father. Tell him to talk to my father."

Anna shook her head. "I don't think he'll listen to me. He doesn't even like me to talk about it."

"Well, talk to your mother, then. Maybe she'll speak to him."

"Maria, I don't know. My mother is the same as my father. She always warn me not to say anything, neither." She paused for a moment. "I guess I not used to asking for anything."

Maria looked over at the little ABCer sitting quietly on the bench forming the letter *A* with a stick in a patch of dirt.

"Is Miss James here?" Maria asked.

"Oh, yes. She still inside."

Slowly more girls gathered in the yard. Maria spotted Elizabeth and Diana talking with their friends. She adjusted her dinner basket and folded her arms. "Now, Anna. The wonderful idea I had that will really help you is that I'm going to start a sewing circle, and we're going to sell what we make and raise money for you."

"But no one can know, Maria."

"We can raise the money and give it to the antislavery society. That's why you should tell your father to go to the meeting. They're having one this Saturday." She looked expectantly at Anna, waiting for her to smile and thank her.

Anna looked worried. "I don't know, Maria. I don't

think it will work. We'll probably have to run and hide again."

"I'm going to start a sewing circle anyway." Maria threw her head back and folded her arms, her dinner basket swinging to and fro. She was just like Miss Truth.

As the church bells struck nine, Miss James and Headmaster Clark both stepped out of the girls' building. Everyone lined up. Maria wondered whether he had told Miss James how she'd helped the monitors.

As she stood in line behind Sarah, she thought about the sewing circle. She had to do it. And it would be a way to go to a meeting. After all, if she and the sewing circle raised money, they'd have to present it at a meeting. All she had to do was to try to figure out a way to get Anna to tell her parents about the abolitionist meeting.

"Hey, where are you, Maria? You seem so far away."

She jumped as Sarah tapped her on the shoulder. "A sewing circle. I want to start a sewing circle."

Sarah felt Maria's forehead with the back of her hand. "Are you okay? You're not ill? I think you're a little feverish."

Maria knocked her hand away. "No, I'm not ill. I'll tell you about it later."

As they entered the building, Sarah almost bumped the girl ahead of her. "But you hate to sew."

"I'll tell you about it later."

Maria smiled to herself as she looked around the classroom. They were all in their places sitting as still as statues. The two girls with the frilly pantalets were absent, and so was the monitor for the third form. Several of the other girls whose attendance was usually irregular were also absent. Everyone, though, who lived on Cedar Lane was there.

Miss James stood at her podium and looked around at the girls.

"Girls, I heard that everything went well yesterday, except that some of you were restless.

"Before we begin, I know that most of you realize that a petition was made to City Hall to ask that the city not go through with plans to build a park here. We do not know what will happen in the future." She hesitated and cleared her throat before continuing to speak. "In the meantime, we have to make the most of our time together." She paused again and rested her eyes on each of them.

"So, girls, we must be thankful for what we have now, and pray to God for strength to face the future. You girls are fortunate that you are not like your colored sisters in the slave states. Those girls will never see the inside of a schoolhouse."

From where she sat, Maria thought that she saw Anna twitch.

"Learn all that you can. You know someday you might be called upon to instruct, and teaching is a wonderful profession for women. So we will make the most of where we are now, who we are now, and what we have now."

A girl raised her hand. "Miss James, where are Melinda and Alice and ..."

Miss James raised her hand, stopping her. "They have

all moved. And that's why I said we have to make the best of the time we have here together."

Without thinking, Maria clapped, and the other girls followed suit. At that moment, Miss James made her feel strong and hopeful, just as Miss Truth had.

Miss James turned a little red. "Oh, girls, now you flatter me." She put her hand to her heart. "But this is just a life lesson, girls. Remember, our strength is in the Lord."

Maria raised her hand.

Miss James nodded. "Yes, Maria?"

"Miss James. Can we start a girls' abolitionist sewing circle?"

Everyone, including Miss James and even the little ABC pupils, stared at Maria with a shocked expression. One girl nearly fell off her seat. Then Miss James crossed her arms over her chest and said, "Maria, Maria. What a wonderful idea!" Still, she looked puzzled and confused. "When I was a girl, we had a junior antislavery society; but, Maria, I had no idea you girls would be interested in starting one. Since this was your idea, you will talk to the girls just before we have lunchtime dismissals, and tell them what you have in mind. In the meantime, girls, we'll begin our morning as usual with our Scripture lesson, and then I will announce the promotions."

Maria realized that she hadn't even thought about a plan—all she had was a wonderful idea.

Each time Miss James declared a student promoted, the girls all squealed with delight, as if they were surprised.

Finally, Miss James had to stop, clapping her hands to

quiet them. "Girls, what has gotten into you this morning? Why are you so giddy?"

The older girls seemed as if it didn't matter to them whether or not they'd moved to the next level, which would be the Class of Merit and monitor. Maria knew that she would remain where she was because of the sewing.

Sarah and four other senior girls were promoted into the Class of Merit. Sarah's ciphering had improved. All of the girls from the youngest group, except the new ABCer and Anna, moved up to the first form, where they would now learn one- and two-syllable words. It seemed to Maria that she, Anna, and the new ABC pupil were the only students who stayed in the same places.

The final blow came when Elizabeth was promoted to the eighth form, Maria's level. But Maria was not angry with sweet, perfect Elizabeth. She just wanted to get the sewing circle started. While she automatically went through the Tuesday morning routine, her mind was actually on what she would tell the girls.

At about ten minutes before lunchtime, Miss James called Maria to the front of the classroom. "Maria, now come and tell us how you wish to organize the sewing circle."

Maria's hands were sweaty as she stepped down to the front of the room, but she held her head high and kept her back straight, and no one could tell that her stomach flitted around like a flock of birds. Even the brave and determined get nervous.

Miss James let Maria come up and stand at the

podium. Glancing at Anna, who kept her head down, Maria tried to settle her nerves.

"Ah, good—good morning, girls . . ." Maria could not look at Diana or Elizabeth. They all stared at her, and it made her feel even more self-conscious than she already was. It had been so different yesterday, when she was commanding them to be quiet.

"I, uh, think we should have a girls' sewing circle to help the abolitionists. There are small children who . . . small children who need our help." How she wished that she could just say what was on her mind. Tell them what the situation was. Tell them about a girl right in their midst who was a fugitive slave, who was someone's piece of property. A girl who needed to be free, and whom they could help.

She sighed deeply and began again. "Slavery is a cruel and awful thing. If we lived in the Southern states, we wouldn't be in a classroom. We probably wouldn't be with our mothers and fathers. We wouldn't be free. There are girls just like us who are treated like property. I think we should do our part to help free our sisters and brothers in the slave states. Just because we are young, that doesn't mean we can't do our part."

One girl raised her hand. "Where will we meet?"

"Well, I . . . I was thinking. I . . ." Maria looked at Miss James, who sat behind her desk as if she, too, were waiting for an answer from Maria. "I . . . I . . . Perhaps we could meet on Friday afternoon here in school? That way, everyone who wants to could join." She looked at Miss

James again. "Maybe on Friday, an hour before school ends—and I will ask my mother if we can have a Saturday meeting at my house."

Miss James nodded. "Yes. Certainly you can meet here on Fridays. You can meet for the entire afternoon. You girls did so well for your examinations, what better way to finish off the school year?"

Maria cleared her throat. "Now, I was thinking we could arrange it so that someone reads for our entertainment while we sew."

Sarah smiled slightly and raised her hand. "So, who will be the reader?"

"Well, I don't mind doing it. But whoever wants to."

Maria would have loved to be the reader, but she didn't want them to think she was doing this for herself. She looked at her schoolmates and tried to smile and speak in a cheery voice. "Who would like to be a member of the sewing circle?"

Every ABCer raised her little hand. Sarah, Diana, and Elizabeth raised their hands. Maria tried not to let her disappointment show. Anna, of all people, kept her hand down. Maria hadn't planned on this. The ABC pupils could only make little samplers. How much money could they raise from those?

Miss James smiled at the youngest students. "We'll organize our own little group, dears. And you girls go home in the afternoon, remember?"

Maria was terribly disappointed. *What is wrong with these girls? Don't they care?* she thought.

And why wouldn't Anna join?

Sitting in the back of the room, Little Miss raised her hand. "What will the name of the group be?"

Once again, Maria was disappointed. She had thought Little Miss was raising her hand to say she'd join the group. "I . . . I hadn't thought about that yet," she said. She didn't like feeling so nervous. She tried to sound firmer, and she held her head a little higher. She tried to stand tall, like Miss Truth. "As Miss James said, we only have now. This might be the last time we do a special task together."

The church bells rang twelve times, breaking the complete silence. Maria felt like a fool.

⅔ CHAPTER 23 ⅔

A CHANGE OF HEART

THE GIRLS SCATTERED around the room with their dinner baskets. Anna quietly took hers and walked back to her usual seat. Sarah sat down next to Maria.

"We're going outside after we eat," she said.

Maria took her bread out of the basket. "You and my two sisters are the only girls who volunteered to be in the circle."

Diana, her eyes sparkling with excitement, rushed over to them before Sarah could answer. "I'm going to be in the sewing circle, so I'll have lunch with you and Sarah now."

This was not the sewing circle Maria had imagined, with a little pest like Diana. But she tried to be patient. "No, Diana. You have lunch with Amy. I have to talk to Sarah."

"About what? The sewing circle?"

"No, it's about our arithmetic exercises. You'll sit

with us when we have the sewing circle."

That seemed to satisfy Diana, and she walked away.

"Sarah, why didn't any of the girls join?"

Sarah shrugged her shoulders. "Some of them are angry with you over yesterday. Because you threatened them."

Maria chomped down on the bread so hard that she almost bit her tongue. "I didn't threaten them. They were being rude. And I didn't tell on them. And what's wrong with the senior girls and the monitors? Why won't they join?" Maria looked over at Little Miss, who sat at one of the tables with Naomi and some of the other monitors. "I helped them."

Sarah shrugged her shoulders again. "Maybe they didn't want your help."

Maria chewed angrily. "I'll never do it again." She turned her attention to Anna, who remained at her seat in the front of the room instead of eating with Sarah and Maria. "I have to talk to Anna. She's so shy, you know. I don't understand why she doesn't want to be in the circle."

Sarah looked down at Anna. "I don't think she's shy. She spoke up for you yesterday, didn't she?"

Sunlight streamed into the room along with the shouts of the boys playing ball. The girls began to drift outside. Sarah stood up. "Let's finish eating in the yard."

"No. I have to talk to Anna. I'll meet you later."

Maria took her lunch basket and walked over to Anna.

Before Maria could say anything, Anna said, "Maria, why you do this? I don't want anyone to know this is for me."

Maria had never seen her so angry before. She hadn't

meant for this to happen. "You heard what I said, Anna. I didn't say anything about you."

"The girls don't seem to care anyway."

Maria folded her arms. "If they knew the reason . . ."

Anna cut her off. "But you can't tell them."

"You know I would never tell. But I want to have a sewing circle anyhow. If you join, then there'll be five of us." She thought for a moment. "If no one wants to join, then I'll be my own sewing circle."

"You alone is not a circle, ma'am. More like a straight line," Anna said, and they both laughed.

"If you join, then there'll be two straight lines. That's why I asked Miss James to let us have it in school."

"I don't even have sewing supplies, except for the sampler and the thread and needle Miz James so kindly give me."

"My mother will give you supplies."

"I don't know, Maria. I just don't know." She shook her head.

"Anna, after school. Walk up the hill with us. My mother will give you all the supplies you need and straw to make a basket with. Anna, please join us."

Anna lowered her eyes, and Maria remembered. "Your mother will be waiting for you."

"Yes."

"Well, your mother can come with you to Mama's store. My mother would be happy to see her."

"No. We have to go right home. We have the laundry to do."

"I'll get the supplies for you, then. You'll need straw for a basket—and what do you want to make?"

Anna finally met Maria's gaze. "I like to make a quilt, but I can't beg from your mother."

"It's not begging. Now, tell me what you need for a quilt."

"Any kind of scraps of muslin and thread." Anna brightened a little. "Maybe some white cotton and blue and green, if your mother has it and she doesn't mind."

"That's settled, then. I'll get everything you need. If you join, then we can show these girls that we can have a sewing circle without them."

Anna stared at her friend and began to shake her head. "You know, ma'am, you is like a millstone around my neck." Then she smiled. "You so determined. I'll join."

"Oh, Anna, that's so wonderful! I knew you'd have a change of heart. Now you just need to figure out a way to get your father downtown."

"I haven't figured out how yet."

Maria tilted her head to one side and took another bite of bread. "Just open your mouth, ma'am, and tell them."

"Maria, you don't understand." She lowered her voice. "They don't want to talk about what happened to us and where we from. Even if it's only us in the room, they still won't mention anything, fearing the walls have ears."

Anna wasn't the only person who would have a change of heart that day. After they ate, Anna and Maria walked outside. Some of the boys had thrown off their jackets, and a group of girls who were playing Wash My Lady's Dresses had taken off their cloaks. The warm afternoon hinted at spring.

As soon as they appeared outside, Byron, almost on the other side of the yard, called Maria. "The more you beat up that boy it seem the more he like you," Anna giggled.

Maria grinned. "Let's show these boys how we can outrun them."

"I like that game," Anna said.

Just as they started to race over to the boys, Little Miss approached them, her nose in the air. "I thought of something you said, that this might be the last time we're together. And since you helped me, I'll join the circle, too."

Maria was so shocked she had to sit down on the nearest bench. "You? You want to join?" She didn't want to sound too excited. "Oh, thank you. I'm so glad."

Little Miss sat next to her. "But you have to find a name."

Anna remained standing and rolled her eyes at Little Miss.

"Yes, ma'am," Anna mumbled.

Little Miss didn't hear her and stood up and walked away.

"Anna," Maria said, "I bet everyone else will follow her."

When they went back to class that afternoon, Maria put more effort than ever into working on her shirt. She half finished one sleeve, and while the stitches were not as perfect as Anna's, they were neat.

When they got home that afternoon, Diana burst into

the store first. "Mama, Maria is starting a sewing circle and wants to have a meeting here on Saturday."

Mama stopped slicing a block of cheese. "What? Maria? A sewing circle?"

Maria sighed. "Diana, this is my news, and you're not giving me a chance to tell it."

Elizabeth grinned. "It's such shocking news, she couldn't wait."

Simon came running in. "Maria, is it time for my lesson?"

"Simon, you go back outside and play for a little while. I'll call you in shortly," Mama said. She turned to Maria. "What is this about a sewing circle?"

And as Maria explained wanting to start a sewing circle to help the abolitionist cause, she saw Mama staring as if she didn't believe her. She dared not mention that she wanted to read to the girls as they sewed.

"Maria, I can't convince you to knit a pair of socks, and now you want to start a sewing circle? I think this circle is just a social event, because you can't go to the meeting with your Papa and Moosa on Saturday."

"We had our first meeting this afternoon at school, and I worked very hard on my shirt, Mama."

"Well, that shirt should've been completed a long time ago, and it's because of the shirt that you're in trouble." Mama wrapped the slices of cheese she'd just cut. "You can meet in school, which will give you and the other girls enough time to make things to sell to raise money. I think it's a fine idea, Maria, but you're going to have your own sewing circle here with me and your sisters, tonight and every night."

She turned her back to Maria and took the jar of cinnamon off the shelf. "You can't devise these clever tricks to get out of doing what you're supposed to do."

Maria felt heat rising from her feet all the way up to her head as she leaned close to Mama. "Mama, please. I'm really not trying to trick you." If only she could have told Anna's secret.

Mama took a scoop of cinnamon and put it in a small paper bag, then folded the bag. "This Saturday is laundry day, so I think you'll be too busy for a sewing circle anyway. If it rains, there will be bloomers and sheets hanging all over the house." Her bright eyes bored into Maria. "And you know, Maria, we are a family, and we all have to help to take care of one another. We have to make articles for the store and for your Papa to sell."

"Mama, I will make everything I need to make for you and Papa, even when I have the sewing circle. I'll do extra sewing so I'll have something to sell, too."

"Maria, I don't know how this idea came to you. Why are you so determined about this?"

"Because I want to be like you, Mama. I want to have a sewing circle like you had when you were thirteen."

Mama was silent for a moment as she stared into Maria's moist eyes.

"Maria, I will let the girls meet here once. And if you do not knit three pair of socks next week and complete your shirt perfectly and get promoted to the Class of

Merit, as you should be by then, no sewing circle for you. The abolitionists will have to do without your good works."

Maria grabbed her mother, almost lifting her off her feet, and spun around with her in a crazy circle. "Oh, Mama, thank you, thank you! I promise, I'll be perfect."

Mama tried to get out of Maria's grasp. "Stop your foolishness."

"Mama, can I give Anna straw to make a basket for school and some sewing supplies?"

"Give her whatever she needs, and then call Simon in for his lesson."

Maria hurried to the back of the store, where Mama kept straw and extra thread, needles, fabric, and other sewing supplies. The bells tinkled, and the Magpie entered the store.

"Hello, Catalina. I came for the cheese and cinnamon. I need two eggs. Have you read the papers yet today? People further down the hill are selling their property, and the constable is throwing the tenants out of their homes."

Maria wouldn't listen. She was happy at that moment and didn't want to spoil it. She picked out various pieces of material. "Mama said yes. We can have the sewing circle here on Saturday," she said to Elizabeth.

"That's good, Maria. It'll be fun." Elizabeth glowed.

Diana clapped her hands. "I'm going to make some more pantalets."

If they only knew how important their sewing was, Maria thought.

CHAPTER 24

STITCHING FOR FREEDOM

THE EXCITEMENT MARIA had felt on Monday had just about disappeared by Friday. The only good thing that had happened that week was that Miss James had let her help Anna with the alphabet. Anna was up to *H* and *I*. Maria had continued to prod the girls who hadn't joined. "This might be the last time we can do something important together. We can help the abolitionists."

None of the girls said no outright—just "Maybe," "I'll think about it," "My mother can't afford more sewing supplies," or "I live too far away to come to your house."

And Maria would answer, "Yes or no makes more sense than maybe. Why do you have to think about something so important?" and "My mother will give you supplies," and "If you can't come on Saturday, then just come on Fridays at school."

By Thursday, Emily and Amy had joined, but Maria was still disappointed, because they weren't senior girls or members of the Class of Merit. She wanted the older girls. The articles had to be made quickly and well in order to be of help to Anna.

When Maria left her house on Friday morning, she was still wondering whether anyone else would join. She was surprised that the girls hadn't followed Little Miss.

The heavens opened up that Friday morning, drenching the Peters sisters as they crowded together under the same umbrella. They walked carefully down a very muddy Cedar Lane.

"I didn't want to get out of bed this morning," Diana said. "I just wanted to hear the rain beating on the roof."

Elizabeth looked out at the gray trees and sky. "You have to come to school today. Maria is having her sewing circle."

"Are you really going to sew, Maria?" Diana giggled.

"Of course I am."

"But I bet you don't want to," Diana said, her eyes gleaming playfully.

They passed the cedar grove near the Magpie's house. The cedars were the only green among the bare gray trees and bushes. "If you don't behave yourself, I won't let you be in it. It's for the senior girls, anyhow," said Maria.

"But I sew better than ..."

Elizabeth stopped her before she could finish. "No

fussing. Maria's sewing circle is going to help somebody be free."

Maria almost stopped walking. *Does Elizabeth know about Anna?* she wondered. "Who do you think it will help?" Maria asked.

"I don't know. Someone maybe like the man from Maryland Papa told us about," Elizabeth said.

"Yes," Maria said, "it will help someone."

The school yard was desolate. Everyone was inside, out of the pouring rain.

They hurried into the building. As they went through their Friday morning routine, she recognized that more girls were absent. One was Melissa, the writing monitor, who didn't live on Cedar Lane, but in a house further down the hill from the school; the other girls were in the second and third forms. The empty desks were multiplying. As Naomi wrote out the ciphering exercises on the blackboard, Maria whispered to Sarah, "I wonder why Melissa is absent."

Sarah shrugged her shoulders. "She lives on Sixtieth Street. Maybe her family had to move." Sarah leaned closer to Maria. "My father read in the paper that people who rent houses have already started moving."

Maria copied the exercises onto her slate. "We own our houses, so the city can't make us move. The petitions will stop them."

Sarah started copying, too, and then stopped and whispered, "Maria, why do you really want to have a sewing circle?"

Maria didn't look at her. "I have no reason, except that I want to help the abolitionists."

Sarah stared at her very closely. "It doesn't fit right for you. Suppose I started a ciphering circle?"

Maria giggled. "Now, that's the silliest thing you've ever said."

Unfortunately, the rain never completely stopped, so the girls ate inside, and a restless feeling spread throughout the room. Maria felt it and began to doubt that the sewing circle would be able to make a difference for Anna, especially if Anna's parents didn't attend a meeting.

But suppose Anna and I went, and we both told Anna's story? she wondered.

The ringing church bells startled her. Suddenly, Miss James walked over to her. "Maria, you girls can form your group in the back while everyone else stays with me."

Maria, Elizabeth, Diana, Sarah, Little Miss, Amy, and Emily went to the back of the room. Maria glanced back at Anna, who looked as though she were going to stay where she was. But then she rose from her desk slowly and joined them.

"Well, Maria, this is your sewing circle, so now you have to tell us what to do," Little Miss said.

Every girl had her sewing basket. Maria stood in front of the tables where the girls sat and ignored Little Miss. She was trying to be a pain, she thought. "Well, girls, I thought this would be a good way for us to raise money for the antislavery cause."

Little Miss raised her hand. "So, have you thought about what you want us to make? Have you thought about how we will sell what we make? Have you . . ."

Maria wanted to cuff her, but Little Miss was very good at sewing. She put up her hand, silencing her. "I thought of all of that. As Miss James said, we'll have a spring frolic next month. So that means we must have something to sell by then. We should make practical things that people need."

Little Miss raised her hand again. "Well, have you thought of a name for us?" she asked.

"Yes. I have. Stitching for Freedom. If you don't like it, we can think of something together and vote on it."

Little Miss folded her arms and closed her eyes, as if she were thinking very hard.

Sarah said, "I like it."

The others agreed, and Anna said, "It sounds perfect."

Diana said, "I'm going to make a pair of pantalets just like the ones I wear on Sunday, with rows and rows of ruffles."

The girls chuckled.

"I'll knit a shawl," Sarah said.

Little Miss pursed her lips and said in a very proper voice, "I will make a very special dress that should bring in a lot of money."

Amy, the little girl in Diana's form, said, "I'll make as many dolls as I can. Dolls from different countries."

"That's not practical," Little Miss said, before Maria or anyone else could answer.

Maria closed her fist tightly. She turned to Amy. "Dolls are practical. Little girls love dolls. Somebody's mother or father will buy them." She stared at Little Miss, silently daring her to say something else. But that didn't work.

"So, Maria, what will *you* make?" Little Miss asked.

That was the one thing Maria had *not* thought of. "I have a shirt to sew. I'll finish my shirt. But someone has to be a reader to entertain us as we work. Who wants to be a reader this time?"

"I just want to sew my pantalets," Diana said, rummaging through her basket.

No one volunteered to read.

Little Miss stared at Maria with a knowing smile.

"Okay, if no one wants to read, then I will," Maria said.

"Maria, I don't think you're serious. How can you form a sewing circle and not sew?" Little Miss asked, sounding exactly like Miss James.

Sarah covered her mouth to hide her laughter.

"Okay, then," Elizabeth said, "I'll read."

But Maria didn't want her to read; that would have meant wasting her sewing talent. And then she had an idea. "Wait, Wait. Anna will tell us a story to entertain us."

Anna's face was an embarrassed blank. "Maria, what story? . . . You . . ."

"The tailypo story, Anna. The girls will love it."

"Yes. Anna. Tell us the story," Elizabeth said.

"You'll laugh at me. You think I'm stupid."

"If anyone laughs at you and not the story, then I'll box her ears," Maria warned.

Diana said excitedly, "Tell us the tailypo story."

Anna, still looking embarrassed, nodded. She took the large piece of white calico that she'd gotten from Mama out of her sewing basket, along with a piece of green material, and began to tell the story.

Little Miss acted as though she were more interested in the piece of lace she was examining.

When Anna had finished, Sarah said, "That's the best story I ever heard."

Diana's smile was wide. "Anna, I want to hear it again."

Anna repeated the story. This time, when she came to the part where the animal started wailing, "Tailypo, give me back my tailypo," the girls said it along with her, including Little Miss.

The students sitting in the other part of the room looked over at them. Miss James looked up from her desk. "Girls, are you sewing?"

"Yes, Miss James," said Little Miss. "Anna has just entertained us with a delightful story."

Miss James looked surprised. "Anna? Oh, very nice."

When school ended, Amy moaned, and Emily said, "I don't want to leave."

Maria took her time putting away her sewing and going to the closet for her cloak. She hoped that some of the other girls would come over to her and tell her that they'd changed their minds about joining the circle. But everyone just rushed out, as they usually did on Fridays.

Anna waited for her, though, and they walked out of the building together. "The circle was nice, Maria," she said. "Thank you."

Maria didn't want to say that the circle was too small to be of much help.

CHAPTER 25

A SPECIAL GUEST

L ATE ON SATURDAY afternoon, Maria walked from the kitchen into the sitting room and hoped that there'd be enough seats for everyone. At least four of them could sit on the couch. Two girls could sit on the large chairs, and someone else could sit on the ottoman. She'd bring in the chairs from the kitchen if need be.

Though she'd washed her face, combed her hair, and changed her dress, she still felt as if her face were sweaty and her hair frizzy from a day of pounding and scrubbing clothes and sheets in steamy hot water.

She made sure that the newspapers, along with Simon's toys and Moosa's books, were neatly put away. At four o'clock, Maria, Diana, and Elizabeth looked at one another.

"Suppose no one comes," Diana said, taking a piece

of white cotton out of her basket.

"Well, then, we'll just have our own sewing circle," Elizabeth said, picking up her knitting needles.

"That's what we have anyway, every Saturday, except we're not stitching for freedom." Maria tried to sound happy, as though it didn't matter whether anyone came.

Dukie sat in front of the fireplace, and Simon raced into the sitting room, stirring him up.

"Simon, I'm having company, so you can't play in here tonight," said Maria.

"Is Diana going to play with me?" Simon asked.

"No, she's in the sewing circle, too."

He folded his little arms and stamped his foot. "I want to be in it, too."

"It's only for girls, Simon," Maria said.

"Well, Dukie and I can play in the back quietly with my toys."

Maria tried not to laugh. "You and Dukie never play quietly. He's just a dog. What does he know about playing quietly with toys?"

"I'll play with my toys by myself, in my corner of the room," he said, pouting.

Diana, sitting daintily on the ottoman, said, "You're just a little boy, and this is for girls. You can't be with us."

Simon opened his mouth wide. It was a while before a sound came out, but when it did, it was a loud howl filled with hurt.

Maria turned to Diana. "You know he loves you best; now, why did you speak so harshly to him?"

Diana went to Simon and hugged him. "I'm sorry, Simon. I didn't mean to hurt your feelings."

Mama rushed into the room. "What is the matter, Simon? Girls, what have you done to him?"

Suddenly, Dukie raced to the door and began to bark, while Simon continued to cry. Maria followed the dog to the door. There was Little Miss, who immediately frowned. "Oh, such a racket," she said, as Dukie barked and jumped on her for a little petting. She backed away with a disgusted look on her face, and Maria was immediately sorry that she had let Little Miss be in the circle, even if she was the best with a needle.

She probably came just to criticize, Maria thought.

"Hello, Amelia," Mama said, and she turned to Simon, wiping his face with her apron. Maria grabbed Dukie by the scruff of the neck and pulled him away from Little Miss.

"Tie him up in the kitchen," Mama ordered, "otherwise he'll jump on every girl who walks in the door."

"He's spoiled and likes to be petted," Elizabeth said as she led Little Miss into the sitting room. Little Miss sat down in Papa's big chair and looked uncomfortable. "I think it's going to rain, Maria. I don't know how many girls will come."

"Well, most of the girls live around here, and a little rain shouldn't stop them. They won't melt." Maria glanced at the clock before she sat down on the sofa. It was almost four thirty, and she was beginning to think that this sewing circle was a terrible idea. Where was Sarah? She lived just across the road.

Little Miss crossed her legs. "So, I wonder if anyone else is coming? I don't know how much money we can raise if no one is in the circle but us."

Elizabeth said hopefully, "I think the others will come. We're all so close by."

Little Miss scanned the room again. "Maria, did you plan an entertainment for the circle?"

Maria thought that it would be ridiculous and rude to cuff someone who was a guest in her house, but she was tempted. "Someone can read," she said drily as she picked up her knitting needles. "Elizabeth, you read."

"But I want to work on the shawl I'm going to knit."

"I'm using this for the pantalets I'm making," Diana said to Little Miss, proudly holding up the pink lace she was using for trimming.

Little Miss ignored her, and Maria quickly said, "That's beautiful, Diana."

Maria was on the verge of canceling the meeting, but then she remembered what she'd told Anna, that she'd have a sewing circle of one if necessary. "Lizzie, just do us this favor, just for a while. Then I'll read." Her face lit up. "We'll take turns entertaining each other. Diana can read, too."

Before anyone could answer her, Dukie barked from the kitchen, and Simon went to open the door. Amy, from Diana's form, entered the sitting room, along with Naomi and Sarah. Sarah carried a large platter covered with a white cloth. "Sorry I'm late," she said cheerily. "My mother and I made some cupcakes."

Mama took the platter and put it on the kitchen table. "This was so nice of you and your mother! Thank you."

They all sat down together, and Maria observed that everyone looked very colorful and bright. Not one of them wore her plain school dress and apron.

"What about the entertainment, Maria?" Little Miss asked again.

Sarah said, "I wish Anna were here so we could listen to one of her stories. I don't suppose she's coming."

"She has a longer way to travel," Maria said.

"Where does she live, anyway?" Little Miss asked. No one answered.

Sarah said, "I'll do the entertainment, then. I'll sing."

Everyone moaned, knowing Sarah's reputation for not being able to carry a tune. Maria took charge. "Since this is for the abolitionist cause, and we're junior abolitionists, which is very serious, then we should be serious." She kept talking as she walked to the back of the sitting room where they kept their books. "I will read *The Narrative of Frederick Douglass* for a spell; then Sarah can sing. So, Elizabeth, you can work on your shawl."

Diana frowned. "Just let Sarah sing."

Sarah can't sing, Maria thought.

It would have pained Maria to let anyone else read. That would have left one less person who could make something to sell. It was bad enough that she couldn't even make anything for the circle yet, since she'd first have to knit the three pairs of socks for Papa. She couldn't make the kind of articles the other girls created. So, even though she knew what everyone, including her mother, would think, she read anyway.

Little Miss put on the sleeves of the dress she was making. Diana measured the ruffles on her pantalets, so that they would be evenly placed. Emily was stringing the pink and blue beads that would decorate the purse she'd made. Elizabeth knitted her shawl. Sarah sewed the seams of the plain dress that she had already started. Amy had a basket full of rags; she removed a handful and began to form the round shape of a head for the first doll she'd create. Little Miss stared at her for a moment and then shook her head as if to say, "How silly."

They worked quietly; Maria's smooth, clear voice totally absorbed them.

Suddenly, Dukie barked again, and Simon ran to the door. Maria heard her mother say, "Go in the room, Anna. Let me take your wet cloak. The girls are in there. Mrs. Holmes, have a cup of tea."

As Anna entered, Maria made room for her on the couch.

"Oh, I'm so glad you're here, Anna."

"I have to tell you what happen later," Anna whispered.

"Hello, Anna!"

"Hi, Anna."

"Anna, we were just talking about you."

They all smiled in her direction, as if she were a special guest. Anna pulled out the quilt she was making. Maria noticed that there was a lot of blue material on top and some pieces of white cloth over the blue, resembling clouds.

Once they settled down again, Anna stopped sewing and listened to Maria read. Maria looked up from the page she was reading and realized that Frederick Douglass's story was Anna's story as well. When she finished the first chapter, Amy said, "I didn't understand."

"I didn't understand it, either," Diana said.

Maria stood up. "Let's take a rest for a moment and eat some cupcakes." It was about seven o'clock when the girls walked into the kitchen. Mama was standing by the stove ironing, and Mrs. Holmes was folding clothes for her. They were both laughing, and Maria realized that this was the first time she'd ever heard Mrs. Holmes laugh. Mama wasn't looking at the clock as she usually did on Saturdays when Moosa and Papa were downtown.

As the girls ate and talked in the kitchen, Maria pulled Anna aside, and they went into the sitting room and sat down on the sofa.

"I'm surprised your mother brought you. But I'm so glad."

"Well, I tell my mother about the sewing circle, and she say if we finish the laundry she bring me to your house. She say you and your family are righteous people."

They heard the girls laughing in the kitchen, with Diana's voice louder than everyone else's.

Anna went on, "I tell her that you told me your father and brother went to the meeting, and I tell her how Miss Truth get the people to give money to help that poor man what was kidnapped, and she say, 'What that have to do with us?' And I say maybe Papa could tell them about me, and they would pay to help free me.

"She get angry at first and say, 'That woman have no right to own none of us. We ain't cattle. Why should we pay? You our child, not hers. And we not begging people. We pay for our freedom and you our child. And remember what happen the last time we trust someone.'"

Maria sighed. "Anna, I wish we could each take your father by the arms and drag him to the meeting."

"You and me dragging my father? Oh, Maria, even the man who own us couldn't drag my father anywhere. That's why he rent him out." She started giggling.

Little Miss walked into the room. "What's so funny, girls? Let all of us laugh," she said, sitting down in Papa's chair.

Before Maria could think of an answer, Diana rushed in and said, "Anna, tell us the tailypo story again, and I'll act it out."

Anna agreed. As she recited, Diana made all of the motions, lying back in the chair as if she were sleeping, opening up her eyes wide and biting on her fingers. The girls laughed so much they couldn't sew. Even Maria couldn't get angry with her for showing off.

When the clock struck eight they gathered their sewing and prepared to leave. The rain had stopped, and a bright, full moon lit their way. Little Miss said to Maria, "Will your mother let us come back next week?"

"I think so." *If I finish the socks I'm knitting,* Maria thought.

"This is the best sewing circle I've ever been in," said

Little Miss with a flounce of her skirt. "And I've been in many of them."

Maria smiled. Little Miss was the last person she would have expected a compliment from.

As Maria watched Anna and her mother walk down the road, though, she had little hope that this sewing circle of only eight girls could help Anna. Anna's father had to talk to Papa or go to the antislavery meeting. Maria decided that she had to come up with a plan to get them there.

CHAPTER 26

A STRANGER

MARIA WAS PROUD of the way she chopped wood almost as well as Moosa. She liked the feeling of strength as she raised her arms and brought the ax down on the small logs, splitting them with one stroke.

She split a log that Moosa had already cut. This was one thing she could do: make the logs shorter or longer. It was up to her, she thought, as she continued to split the logs into small pieces that would fit comfortably in a person's arms. She had a choice about the logs, but not about much else.

Even though she'd started the sewing circle, Anna and her family might move away before the girls completed anything to sell. Neither Anna or her parents had been in church the previous day. A thought crossed Maria's mind: Suppose Anna and her parents had actually left?

Everyone might move away if the petitions didn't keep the city from taking their property. Therefore, Maria took great pleasure, especially this morning, in deciding how long or short the logs would be.

When Maria reached school later that Monday morning, she saw all of the girls who'd been to her house on Saturday. She was relieved to see Anna, standing near the front of the girls' building, talking to Sarah and Naomi. The new little ABC student who had attached herself to Anna stood there as well.

Maria was surprised at the big smile and wave she received from Little Miss, who sat with another monitor on the bench.

Maria walked up to Sarah, Anna, and Naomi.

"Hi, Maria," Sarah said. "I was just telling Naomi how much fun we had on Saturday."

"It would have been even better if more girls had joined," Maria said, staring at Naomi, who avoided her eyes.

"Emily told me she had a good time. But you know those little girls. Everything is a good time to them," Naomi said.

"It was a good time," Anna said.

When Naomi and Sarah began talking to another girl, Anna lowered her voice. "It the first time anyone ever invite me anywhere."

Anna and Maria walked away from the girls' building toward the back of the school yard and nearer to the church, and sat on a bench.

"I looked for you yesterday in church," Maria said.

"We say a prayer at home, Maria, because my mother had laundry to finish and I had to help her."

"What about your father?"

"He work, too, helping this man clean his—"

"No, I mean, is he going to the meeting? Did your mother convince him?"

Anna sighed loudly, shaking her head. "No one can convince him. He . . ." Anna stopped speaking and pointed toward the church. "Maria, did you see that? A man I never see before 'round here just slip in back of the church."

"It must've been Reverend Arlington," Maria said, squinting, but not really seeing anything.

Anna caught her breath. "No. It's not. It's a stranger, and he creeping around like he looking for someone."

"Oh, Anna, maybe you just imagined . . ."

Anna grabbed her arm, and they walked quickly to the front yard just as Miss James came out of the girls' building. Anna rushed to her place at the head of the line, and Maria walked to the end, stepping into place behind Sarah.

Sarah immediately turned around. "Maria, have you noticed that the number of boys is dwindling?"

Maria looked over at the boys' building, and there seemed to be fewer of them, but all of the boys who lived on Cedar Lane were there. Then Maria noticed something else. A man was walking toward Miss James. Was this the stranger Anna had seen? His eyes never stopped scanning the students as he talked to Miss James. Maria began to have a bad feeling about him.

Miss James and the stranger continued talking near the front of the line. Suddenly, Anna left her place and raced toward Maria.

"What's wrong with her?" Sarah asked.

Anna pulled Maria aside while Sarah kept asking, "What's wrong? What's the matter?"

"It's not your business," Anna hissed at her; Sarah looked hurt.

Maria and Anna stepped away from the line. Anna could barely speak. "The man ask if a girl here named Esther. That's my slave name, Maria. He looking for me."

The church bells rang. Over the sound of the bells, Maria heard Miss James calling, "Anna, Anna, come here a moment, dear."

Without stopping to think, Maria grabbed Anna's hand and they raced out of the school yard. She turned around briefly and saw the man running after them and Miss James, holding up her skirt, walking quickly behind him and calling to both of them. Maria also thought that she heard Diana's little voice shouting after her.

Maria and Anna raced down the swampy, muddy hill as though they were playing a desperate game of Touch. Maria didn't notice the children scavenging or the goats bleating. She and Anna splattered through the muddy ground without heed to the stench from the bone-boiling factories.

A group of men stopped their digging to look at them curiously. And just when Maria thought that she couldn't take another step, she glanced back and saw the man still giving chase. Anna turned toward a jumble of shacks, and Maria followed her.

The small shacks were so close together they almost leaned on one another. A smelly trench filled with water and refuse ran alongside the homes. Anna dashed inside one of the shacks, and Maria followed. Both of them tumbled to the floor, trying to catch their breath.

"Ma'am, we in trouble now," Anna said as they sat on the dirt floor together without taking off their cloaks.

"Where are we?" Maria asked, looking around the room.

"At my house, but my mother isn't here. She must be delivering laundry," Anna said, her chest heaving up and down.

A large bed stood in one corner, and a smaller bed in the other. Both beds had colorful quilts that brightened the bare room.

"We'll wait for her to come home," Maria said, still trying to catch her breath. "When we tell her what happened, maybe she and your father will go and speak at the meeting."

Suddenly Anna looked at Maria and started laughing. "Ma'am, why did you run? No one is chasing you. You 'bout a silly girl sometime."

Maria sat up and folded her arms around her legs. "I don't think it's so silly to stay by a friend's side when she's in trouble." Then she smiled, too. "I guess it was kind of silly. I could've stayed back and explained to Miss James why you ran."

"No. You can't explain for me."

"Why won't you explain for yourself?"

Anna frowned and avoided Maria's eyes. "I guess I could stand there and say, 'I'm not Esther.'"

"Then he'd have to leave. I know Miss James wouldn't make you go with him. And your mother meets you after school. She wouldn't let anyone hurt you."

"He could come back with the law, Maria, and take both me and my mother. The woman who own me give him a description of me and my mother and father."

"How do you know?"

"My mother and father tell me these things. My mother can't read, but she show me the signs always tacked on trees and in the store windows."

Maria's breathing had become more even. She was silent for a moment, then said, "Well, if your mother can't read, how did she know what the signs said?"

Anna got up. "She know the word *runaway*. That's the only word she know, and she taught it to me. The same way somebody taught it to her."

"You never told me."

"I couldn't."

Maria stood up also. "Well, when your mother comes back, we'll explain. And then, she and your father must go to the meeting, Anna. Miss Truth will be there. She could raise the money for you."

"It impossible. We'll be gone from here by tonight. I'll

wait here for my mother." She opened the shutter slightly and peeped out. "I don't see anyone. Maybe he didn't see us turn in here." She closed the shutter and faced Maria. "You free. No one is chasing you down." She pointed toward the school. "Go back up the hill, Maria."

"What will I say to Miss James if I can't tell her why you ran out of the yard?"

"Just tell her that I feel sick and you worry about me and walk me home."

"I'm not leaving you here alone, ma'am," said Maria. She tiptoed to the shutter and, like Anna, opened it slightly. "No one is there, but I still won't leave you." She closed the shutter and sat down on a bench, at a table near the door. "The man knows we're somewhere around here, so I'm staying, too." She folded her arms, and Anna sat down next to her.

Maria was silent for a moment, deep in thought. Then she said, "Anna, it's up to us. We have to do it."

Anna stared at her. "Do what?"

"We have to see Miss Truth."

Anna stared at Maria as if she didn't believe what she was hearing. "You is a mad girl, Maria."

"Maybe I'm mad. We can do it, Anna. We'll walk. Just like Miss Truth did. We'll walk downtown to the church, and we'll get the abolitionists to help you."

"But this is Monday. Suppose nobody there. You tell me they have meetings on Saturday."

"Someone is always at the church." Maria unfolded her arms, and leaned toward Anna. She clenched her teeth. "Anna, this is the only way. My grandma Isabella lives up the street. She goes to the meetings. She knows Miss Truth. Anna, you have to listen. . . ."

Suddenly they heard shouting and dogs barking. Anna opened the shutter so that just a sliver of light showed. She said in a hoarse voice, "He across the road. That same man. And he talking to another man who live around here."

"Can we leave without him seeing us?"

"No. Now the neighbor is pointing to this house."

"But the neighbor doesn't know your story."

"I told you, Maria. The woman who say she own me give out a description of me and my mother and father. And he hear Miss James call my new name. He walking to this yard." She quickly closed the shutter.

"Is your door locked?"

"What lock?"

Maria and Anna, without a word between them, pushed the table up against the door. It seemed that less than a second later, someone tried to open it.

Maria heard a man's voice. "Come back later. They'll be here."

Then, for the first time, they heard their pursuer's voice. "Here is a little something for your help. Don't say anything to them about this."

Maria was afraid to breathe, lest one of the men hear her. The girls faced the door. Finally, Anna tiptoed to the shutter and once again took a quick look. "I don't see him."

"Anna, we have to get out of here and get help. Is the other man there?"

"I don't see him, either."

"Anna," Maria whispered, "even if the man is still there, he can't hold on to the both of us. He didn't look like that big of a fellow, anyway." She smiled. "You know, ma'am, he's not that big. Between you and me we could give him a good cuffing."

"What you think this is, Maria? This isn't Byron and them little schoolboys."

"He can't stop us. We'll walk downtown and get help."

Anna's face was full of doubt. "How much walking is that?"

"Not as much as Miss Truth walked."

"But my mother? What about her?"

"Miss James will tell her what happened."

"But she won't know where we are."

Maria started to suggest that they leave a note for Anna's mother but then remembered that she couldn't read. "Let's leave our baskets. She'll know we've been here and that we're together," she said.

Anna peeked out of the shutter once more. "He's gone, as far as I can tell." She pulled her cloak tightly around her neck. They placed their baskets on the table and moved it enough to get out the door. Anna muttered under her breath, "God help us."

"He will," Maria said.

CHAPTER 27

DOWNTOWN

MARIA AND ANNA left the house, almost crouching as they ran out of the yard. "We go the back way," Anna said. As they raced through other tumbledown yards, they heard someone yell, "Hey, girl. Hey. A man was looking for you."

They ignored the neighbor and kept moving through the yards. "The man pay him for nothing. He telling the world," Anna said.

Sensing that they were still being followed, Maria glanced over her shoulder and saw in the distance the same man who'd been at the school. He didn't call after them but stealthily stalked them like a hunter after his prey.

"He's still following us," Maria said hoarsely.

Dodging goats and pigs and a few barking dogs, they stumbled over rocks and splashed through creeks and brooks. Anna took the lead, and Maria followed her toward a grove of oak trees.

Maria glanced over her shoulder again. The man still followed. Dashing behind the trees, they headed toward a cluster of large rocks that made a cavelike enclosure. They slipped between two boulders and waited there. Maria caught her breath. "Anna, how do you know this place?"

"This the way we come from downtown. My mother and father show me and make me remember it," Anna whispered. "What street are we near? There's a hill back of the boulders, but I don't know the name of the street it go to."

Maria had no idea where they were. When she rode the wagon with Moosa or Papa, they always traveled down the hill from Cedar Lane until they came to Seventy-ninth Street. She was amazed that Anna knew this back way among the rocky stones, hills, and crags of Manhattan. Eventually, the barking died down. They listened for the sound of crunching leaves or small twigs and branches breaking. Silence. Maria was afraid, though, that there was something in the silence.

"I think we should wait a little longer," Anna said.

Maria agreed, and they continued to wait until she couldn't stand it anymore. "Anna, we can't stay here. We have to take a chance." She looked around. "Maybe there's a stick or a stone in case we have to defend ourselves."

"There's nothing. We'd have to step outside to look for something. The man be right on us while we looking."

"Well, come on, then," Maria said. "Let's go!"

They slipped away from the boulders and dashed toward the hill. Maria didn't look back. They continued running steadily, going down a steep hill and to the street.

Anna looked doubtful. "Maria, you think we doing the right thing?"

"This is the only thing we can do, Anna." Maria gazed in the distance toward the swirls of smoke coming out of a cluster of factory buildings. "I think we lost him."

They began their long walk. They stepped over the rocks and tried to avoid the swampy areas when they could. There were so many little creeks that it was impossible to avoid getting wet.

As they walked, they often glanced over their shoulders. There were not as many houses and people here. They saw a few men and some women and even bigger children cutting down small trees for firewood. A scattering of children scavenged for bones and rags. Maria couldn't see the buildings but knew by the putrid scent when they neared a tannery.

When they returned to the paved streets where the horse railroad cars ran, Maria still felt unprotected. They were already at Fiftieth Street. She was glad that her father shined shoes at the depot much farther uptown. There was no chance of running into him.

They followed the tracks of the horse-drawn railroad cars downtown, walking along Sixth Avenue. Maria tried to remain calm, but she couldn't stop looking back.

"Maria, I don't feel right about this," Anna said as they passed a vendor selling candy.

"This is the only way, Anna. We have to see Miss Truth." She pulled her shoulders back and kept the image of Sojourner Truth, walking, before her.

"My mother will be sick with worry. And then when she see me, she . . ."

"She'll be overjoyed."

They neared a small group of trees. Several girls, who probably worked in one of the shops, sat on logs eating.

Anna stopped walking. "I'm going back, Maria. This is foolish. You don't know if that lady is there."

"I feel deep in my heart she is, Anna. Something is telling me that we have to go. Otherwise, you won't be free, and I won't ever see you again if your parents take you away."

Maria spotted the trees and the logs where the girls sat. "Let's just sit over there and rest a moment."

"I don't want to rest, Maria. I going back."

"You need to rest before you go back." She gently pulled Anna's arm, and they both sat down.

Maria tried not to push too hard. She spoke softly. "Anna, I know I'm right. We have to go to the church downtown. I feel sure we'll get help there." She paused for a moment. "Anna, I'm still going, even if you don't."

Maria had never seen Anna look so confused. "But why? I'm not going."

"That's why. I'm going because you won't. I'll go and speak up for you."

Anna lowered her face. "You can't speak for me, Maria."

"Then why won't you speak for yourself?"

"We don't even know if the lady is there."

"We'll never know if we don't look for her. Someone else could be there. Some other abolitionist."

"Something telling me to follow my own mind," Anna said, but she stood up anyway and continued walking with Maria.

When they reached Forty-fourth Street and the Colored Orphan Asylum, Maria waved at the children in the yard as she'd always done when she had been with Papa. She had looked over her shoulder so many times she thought she'd get a crick in her neck.

She felt as though she were dreaming—walking through the streets of Manhattan without her family. She tried to put thoughts of Papa and Mama out of her head. Then she remembered something. Maria didn't have her papers showing that she was free. Mama was always reminding Papa and Moosa to carry them. She didn't want to think about what could happen to her if a kidnapper claimed that she was a runaway.

Instead she thought about Miss Truth walking for her son and other slaves. Did she stop for lunch or to rest? Maria felt that the man was out there, following and watching. Waiting to discover their final destination. Suddenly, there was a commotion behind them. Someone yelled, "Catch them!" and Anna and Maria, in their haste to get away, almost knocked down a vendor's cart.

A woman asked, "What's the matter, girls? Are you all right?" They did not stop to reply.

Not knowing where they were going, they turned down a narrow street lined on either side with ramshackle wooden houses and grocery stores and other small shops. It was the kind of street that the more well-to-do ladies and gentlemen of New York would have hesitated to go down.

They turned into another lane, narrower and darker than the first. The small houses lining either side of the alleyway looked as if they were about to crash around Maria and Anna. Dogs roaming the muddy, unpaved lane barked at them, and several gave chase. A sewer filled with garbage emitted a stench that was worse than the tanneries and bone-boiling plants uptown. Running through an alley off the lane, they came back to Sixth Avenue and almost to the same spot they'd been in before. Several men were arguing with the police and a growing crowd of people. The commotion had nothing to do with Maria and Anna.

So they continued to walk at a steady pace. By the time they reached Thirtieth Street, Maria's feet were throbbing, but she kept the vision of Miss Truth in her mind's eye. She recalled Truth's words: *My children, there is a God, who hears and sees you. That's your power.*

She didn't want to stop, but they had to rest. Everyone seemed an enemy to her, especially the men who glanced their way when they hurried past the growing number of saloons. When they reached Fourteenth Street, Maria's feet were on fire. She and Anna stopped to rest on the steps of a Catholic church.

They walked from Fourteenth Street to Baxter Street.

Maria knew that they were getting closer to Leonard Street. There were even more saloons and people loitering about. The surrounding streets were filled with children, with vendors and women leaning out of windows.

Maria had to try harder to muster her courage as they neared the church. Suppose no one was there? Suppose they were turned away? She glanced at silent, sad Anna.

What is she thinking about? thought Maria. *Is she angry with me? Am I too bossy?*

Finally, when they reached Leonard Street, Maria felt as though she'd walked right out of her muddy boots. Now that she saw the church farther up the block, she prayed that Miss Truth would be there.

CHAPTER 28

SEEKING TRUTH

OCKING ARMS, MARIA and Anna practically held each other up as they trudged along the dirt road. Maria still felt as if she were dreaming. Normally, she'd be riding up Leonard Street with her family. She walked past the familiar stores and shops: McCoy's grocery store, Murray's carpenter shop, and Lloyd's cooper shop with its casks stacked in front. St. Philip's African Church stood only a few feet away from the shops.

Maria looked over her shoulder for the last time that day. She saw Grandma Isabella's house farther up the road and wondered what she would have said if she had known that Maria was walking up the steps to St. Philip's African Church.

They opened the door, and it seemed to Maria that the church was larger than she remembered during those times she'd been there with Grandma Isabella. Perhaps it just seemed larger because the pews and the balcony were empty. A soft light filtered through the stained-glass windows. Anna put her hand over her heart. "Oh, Maria, this is such a big church." Then she added, "But no one's here."

"God is here."

They both sat down in a back pew. "Then I guess we better get to praying long and loud, 'cause no one else can help us, Maria, and we in big trouble now."

Maria looked over at the altar and remembered Miss Truth. She imagined how she had appeared standing in front of the altar of Zion Church that Sunday morning. Maria sighed and rubbed her aching legs. "I believe what Miss Truth told us. I've been praying all the way down here." She gazed around the church. "We didn't come all of this way for nothing, Anna. Miss Truth is here. I just know it.

"See that door over there?" She pointed to a door to the left of the altar. "When I've been here I've seen the deacons going in and out of that door. Maybe there's an office there." She stood up. "I'm going to knock on the door."

"Maria, wait. Maybe we shouldn't . . ."

Maria was already halfway down the aisle; Anna followed her. Maria tapped on the door, lightly at first, then a little louder. Finally, she banged angrily.

Anna stopped her, covering Maria's hand with her own. "Maria, you can't tear down the door in God's house."

Maria dropped her head in shame. "Oh, Anna, I'm so sorry. You were right. Now look at all the trouble I caused. I was so sure she'd be here, or that someone would be here." Tears rolled down her long face.

Anna patted her on the back. "It's okay. You try to help me. At least the man is gone. And my mother probably talk to Miss James by now and so she know why I ran, but she just don't know where I am. We better take the walk back."

Maria shook her head. "No. We'll go to my grandmother. She might even know where Miss Truth is." Images of Sojourner Truth walking tall and brave, and of her grandmother standing defiantly at a window during the race riots, came to her, and she wiped her tears and said, "Miss Truth isn't here, but my grandmother is."

"But then you have to tell her my story, and that's one more person who knows my secret."

Maria turned around and walked with a determined step up the aisle, even though her feet ached. "She can help you. She and my grandfather helped a lot of people."

"No one can help me."

"My grandmother can. Her house is up the street, Anna. You can't go back uptown now."

They left the church and trudged up the dirt road to Grandma Isabella's house. Maria knocked on the door and soon heard Grandma's slow footsteps approaching. Grandma's mouth opened wide. "What's happened, Maria? Something at home? And who is this child?" she asked, staring at Anna.

"This is my friend Anna, and I'm trying to help her."

Grandma Isabella let them in and took a look outside. "Who brought you girls here? Your Papa or Moosa?"

"We walked," Maria said, "all the way from school."

Grandma Isabella reminded Maria very much of Mama as she spun around and raised her voice. "My God, you children walked all the way from uptown? Maria, hang up the cloaks. Sit down at the table, and I'll make you both a cup of tea." The church bells rang six times, and Maria guessed that by now her mother had learned that Maria and Anna had run away from school and that she and Anna's mother were probably besides themselves with worry.

Maria's feet throbbed, but despite the pain and worry, the scent of Grandma's baked bread calmed her down.

As Grandma prepared the tea, she said, "Now, tell me what happened."

"My friend Anna is a . . . is a . . ."

"Maria, whose story is this? Yours or Anna's?"

"Anna's."

"Then she has to tell it."

Grandma turned from the water boiling in the kettle and gazed at Anna's lowered head. She walked over to her and put her soft, wrinkled hand on Anna's shoulder. "Don't be afraid. Tell me what happened. And never hang your head so. I want to help you."

Anna lifted her face, stared into Grandma Isabella's eyes, and seemed to be comforted. She told her story, from the point at which she and her parents left Virginia to the moment just a few hours before, when the stranger came asking for Esther. "I know when he call my name that he is one of them slave-hunters."

Grandma Isabella folded her arms. "You're safe now." She stared at Maria. "Was it your idea to come all the way down here?"

Maria braced herself for a good tongue-lashing. "Yes, Grandma. I thought Miss Truth would be at the church and could help Anna."

"Sojourner Truth travels to many churches and speaks to many people." Grandma Isabella patted Maria's cheek. "You are a foolhardy girl, Maria, but you did exactly what needed to be done."

Images of an angry and worried Mama and Papa tormented Maria. "Grandma, I know Mama and Papa want to kill me, and Anna's mother doesn't know where she is, and . . ."

"When your uncle George comes in from work, I'll send him uptown to tell your parents where both of you girls are. Anna has to stay here, and so do you, because the man saw you with her," Grandma Isabella said. She sat down at the table and faced them. "This is how that fugitive-slave law works. That she-devil of a slave owner who claims to own Anna has set the law on her, so, as far as the law is concerned, she is a fugitive slave. Anyone who helps a fugitive can be arrested, too." She reached for each girl's hand. "Don't you worry. This has been a safe house for many years. Your grandfather and I have helped many a runaway."

Her old eyes regained their sparkle, and the years seemed to fade from her face as she remembered times past. "Everyone we ever helped got away."

"Ma'am," Anna said, "my parents will be sick with worry if they don't know where I am. I can't stay."

"We'll get word to them." Grandma Isabella leaned toward Anna in just the way Maria leaned in when she was determined. "My son-in-law, George, will go uptown and let everyone know who needs to know that you're here. My child, that woman may have a claim on you"—she squared her frail shoulders—"but I can break claims and chains."

At that moment, Maria saw inside her grandmother's heart. Grandmother Isabella was her Truth.

Anna's hands shook slightly as she held her cup of tea. "My father is working in a place call Ulster County."

"Good, good," Grandma said. "He's out of town. We have people who can get a message to him, too."

"But, ma'am, I can't stay here." She began to wring her hands. "Oh, ma'am, I have to leave. I have to."

Anna began to cry. Maria put her arms around her shoulders. "Anna, don't cry. My grandmother will . . ."

Grandma Isabella put her fingers to her lips, and Maria fell silent. "My child," she said softly, "I've been doing this work since before you were born. You will see your parents again, and in a few hours, your mother will know where you are." She patted Anna's hand. "Maria's father will know what to do as soon as he finds out you and Maria are here." She looked deeply into Anna's eyes. "My dear girl, if I let you go back out there it would be like throwing you into a snake pit."

Maria was fearful. She wanted to say something, too, but Grandma had the words.

"You have to stay here. Trust me, Anna. You can't go back uptown now. Maria led you here, but God sent you both. You don't want to fly in God's face, do you?"

"No, ma'am," Anna said.

Grandma stood up and clasped her hands before her. "So, now, let me get you girls supper. I have your favorite, Maria. Codfish."

"Oh, Grandma," Maria tried to joke, "you knew I was coming here." She took another sip of tea. "When do you think Uncle George will come in from work? It breaks my heart knowing how much I'm upsetting Mama. I can't wait to get home."

"Didn't you hear what I said before? You're not going anywhere, Maria," Grandma replied.

"But I thought that I was going back with Uncle George."

Grandma walked toward the cupboard. "You're in as much trouble as Anna. I told you before, the law says that anyone who helps a fugitive can be arrested, too. That man saw you run with Anna, and also heard your teacher call your name. A marshal will be right back at the school looking for both of you tomorrow with a warrant, and if he doesn't find Anna, he'll surely take you."

CHAPTER 29

WAITING

MARIA'S HEAD AND feet throbbed as she listened to Grandma Isabella snoring. She was as loud as Diana. No sounds came from Anna as they all lay in Grandma's four-poster bed. From the time they'd gone to bed, Maria hadn't closed her eyes or shut down her brain. She listened for every sound outside the house.

"Anna," she whispered. "Anna, are you asleep?"

Grandma moaned and turned to one side.

"Anna?" She couldn't understand how Anna could sleep so soundly. "Anna? Are you awake?"

"Yes. I can't sleep."

"I'm getting up."

Both girls quietly slipped out of the bed. The warm, dry socks Grandma had given them didn't protect their feet from the cold wooden floor. And Grandma's nightgowns, far too small for either of them, offered little warmth. They tiptoed out of the room as Grandma continued to snore.

Shivering, Maria put a log on the embers and started a fire. She and Anna huddled under the large quilt that Grandma Isabella kept on the sofa. "I can't sleep, not knowing what's happening and what will happen," she said.

Anna nodded. "My mother. I can't stop thinking how my mother feels."

"Uncle's wagon makes as much noise as Papa's. I've been listening for him, and as soon as I hear him I'm going to go outside and ask him to tell me what happened."

"Are you sure you know how his wagon sound?"

"My auntie's house is right next to this one. We'll hear him."

So they waited and listened as the firelight warmed them and shone on their worried faces. Every time Maria thought that she heard the sound of wagon wheels, she jumped off the sofa and dashed to the window.

She heard the church bells ring ten times. "Anna, he'll be here soon."

"Hope so," Anna whispered. "Maybe he already come and gone."

Maria tried to think of what else she could do to make time pass, to bring her uncle home, and to find out what happened. She felt weak and useless and guilty, too, that her rash act might have caused terrible trouble. "Anna, I'm so sorry. And Miss Truth wasn't even there."

"But your grandmother was. You're a friend. And I never have a friend before."

Then, once again, Maria thought about Sojourner Truth. She wasn't there, but her words still lay in Maria's heart. *My children, there is a God, who hears and sees you. That's your power.*

So Maria prayed: "Dear God, please help my friend Anna. Keep her and her family safe. Help my friend, please." And then she softly sang a song she'd learned in Sunday school.

> *Regard my prayer and answer me;*
> *My every need thine eye can see,*
> *Oh, hear my prayer and answer me.*

Anna followed the tune and repeated the words after Maria. They both sang very softly. And the waiting became a little easier. Just after the church bells tolled eleven times, Maria finally heard Uncle George's wagon and horses coming toward the house.

Maria wrapped herself in another quilt that Grandma had draped over a rocking chair and raced outside in just her stockings. She didn't even notice the little pebbles and stones pressing into the bottoms of her feet. "Uncle George, Uncle George, what happened?" she cried. When she reached the wagon, she was shocked. Anna's mother sat next to Uncle George.

"Have you lost your wits?" he said. "It's cold out here. You should be in bed."

He helped Mrs. Holmes down from the wagon, and she immediately embraced Maria. "My child. You don't know what you did. You saved my girl and us."

Maria was speechless. She looked up at the bright, star-filled sky and said a silent thanks.

When they turned around to walk back to the house, Anna was already racing out the door with the other quilt wrapped around her shoulders. She and her mother hugged and cried.

"Come on, now. Get inside. We don't have a lot of time to tarry," Uncle George said, wiping his forehead with the back of his hand. "Lord, this has been a long night," he mumbled.

When they got inside, Grandma Isabella was in her kitchen. "You girls will catch your death of cold. Get inside here."

She took Mrs. Holmes's hand. "Welcome," she said.

Mrs. Holmes sat down, and Grandma began to build a fire under the stove. "I'll make some tea."

"No fuss, ma'am," Mrs. Holmes said. "Just thank you for taking care of my Anna and helping us."

"Now, miss," Uncle George said to Anna, who was still holding on to her mother, "get dressed, because someone is coming to take you and your mother to a safe house." Anna left, and Maria, still wrapped in her grandmother's quilt, sat down at the table.

"Where is the safe house?" Maria asked.

"If you knew, it wouldn't be safe."

"But why can't they stay here?"

Uncle George winked at Grandma Isabella, as if they had a special secret. "This neighborhood is one of the first places they'll come looking. The marshals and the slave-hunters know the neighborhoods where colored live in Manhattan, either here, downtown, or uptown in your little village. We have a real safe place."

Almost afraid to speak, Maria asked, "Uncle George, what happened? What are my parents saying?"

"When I got uptown it seemed as if everyone on Cedar Lane was in your mother's store. I had to ask her to tell them to leave, except for Mrs. Holmes here and your schoolteacher. Your mother is beside herself. Your father and Moosa and some of the other men had been scouring the woods for you and Anna."

Before Maria could ask another question, Anna's mother spoke up. "I go straight to the school when I don't see my Anna coming to meet me, and when the teacher tell me what happen I knew it was one of them slave-hunters coming after us. I go back to my house thinking Anna and Maria there. I find your baskets, so I know you been there, and you still alive." She handed Maria her basket.

"I see a stranger slinking around, so I walk back to your house and wait with your mother. We hold each other up. I tell her our story. And when your uncle bring the news, me and your mother cry in each other's arms."

Maria heard three taps three times in succession.

"That's them," Grandma smiled.

"Who?" Maria asked.

"The people who are going to help Anna and her mother."

Anna walked back into the kitchen, wearing her cloak. Her face was also long and sad.

Mrs. Holmes took a sip of tea and looked at Maria. "It was good that you and Anna ran. Miss James tell me that the man say to her that Anna is his daughter." Her face was lined and weary. "He lie and say that she had been taken away from him when he was sent to another plantation in Virginia. Miss James say he seem like such a respectable man, she would have let Anna go with him."

Maria glanced at Anna, who then spoke up. "Ma, I know better and wouldn't go no matter what he say. That's why me and Maria run."

"Mrs. Holmes," Maria said, "we wouldn't let that man take her."

Mrs. Holmes stood up and hugged Maria. "You an angel."

Anna and her mother left the house, and Maria, standing by the door, watched sadly as Anna, sitting in the wagon, waved good-bye. Would she ever see her friend again?

CHAPTER 30

LITTLE TRUTH

AT FIRST, MARIA thought she was in bed with Elizabeth and Diana, until she heard Grandma Isabella snoring next to her. Her legs were still achy, a reminder of her long walk the day before. Quietly she left the bed and put on her clothes. She tiptoed down the rickety stairs and went to the privy just outside of the kitchen. She didn't want to go back upstairs to borrow Grandma's brush and perhaps wake her, so she ran her hands through her hair and braided it as best she could.

As she added a log to the smoldering embers in the fireplace, Maria relived the events of the day before. It all seemed like a dream. She made tea and porridge for their breakfast as her head spun with questions and worries: *Where are Anna and her mother? Are Mama and Papa angry with me? When can I go home? Are Lizzie and Diana and Simon asking for me?*

She heard Grandma coming down the stairs and was surprised when the church bells rang ten times. Neither one of them normally slept this late.

"What a night that was, Maria. I hope that you slept after they left." She slowly sat down at the table.

"I think I did. I was so tired." She handed Grandma a bowl of porridge. "Are Anna and her mother safe now?"

"As safe as they'll ever be. Believe me."

"Where are they?"

"I can't tell you that."

Maria poured the tea in the boiling water. "But Grandma, I'm the one who helped her."

"These things are secret. The more you know, the more danger you're in. If you know nothing, you can't tell nothing."

"No one can get information out of me. I know how to stay quiet. Please, Grandma, tell me."

Before Grandma could answer, Maria heard the sound of a wagon clanking noisily as it entered the yard. "That sounds like Papa's wagon," she said, racing to the window. "It's him!" She ran to the door, and if she hadn't been so tall, she would've leaped into his arms the way Simon did; it didn't matter whether or not he was angry with her. She hugged him tightly.

Grandma slowly stood up, walked to the stove and poured the tea. "Solomon, sit down. Have some breakfast with us."

"No, Mother Isabella. I ate already. I just had to

come down here and see how my Maria was doing."

She searched his face. His deep-set eyes looked angry and gentle all at once.

"You're not angry with me, Papa?"

"Of course I'm angry with you. When I think of the trouble you almost got yourself into. Why didn't you stay in school?"

"That man was after Anna. I had to help my friend."

"You knew that she was a slave?"

She lowered her head, just the way Anna did. "Yes, Papa. I knew for a long time."

"Oh, Lord, Maria. Do you know that that makes you guilty of a crime?"

"But I'm not a bad person. I'm not a criminal."

Grandma interrupted. "That fugitive-slave law is hard, Maria. There's no heart in it. You broke it, and that's all there is to it." She sat down.

Maria saw more anger in Papa's dark eyes now. "The law is wrong, but you can't fight it alone. Why didn't you tell me, or Moosa, or your mother?"

"Anna begged me not to. I promised to keep her secret."

Papa sat down at the kitchen table and sighed deeply. Maria sat across from him next to Grandma.

"You took such a chance. That's what upset your mother and me."

"I had to help my friend, Papa."

"You would've helped her by telling me or Moosa." His voice became louder and deeper. "Don't you ever do such a foolhardy thing again. What would we do if we lost you?" His eyes bored into her, and she couldn't look at him.

"Your sisters and brothers are so worried about you. Not to mention your mother. What we would we do without you, Maria?"

Tears trickled down her cheeks. Grandma gently patted Maria's back. Maria wasn't crying because Papa had raised his voice. It was just that she had never known that she was so important to her family.

"When can I go home?" she whispered.

"I don't know. The marshal or that slave-catcher will probably be at the school this morning looking for you and Anna. They'll be down in this neighborhood, too, because they know colored people live in this part of the city and runaways hide here." He handed her a satchel and her sewing basket. "Here, your mother sent this so you have a change of clothing. She wants you to finish your shirt so that you can be promoted."

Maria wiped her eyes with the back of her hand and then began to giggle.

"What's so funny?" Papa asked.

"The shirt. No matter what happens, it follows me," Maria replied.

"Well, better the shirt than the marshal." Papa seemed to calm down a little.

"Maria, drink your tea, now. And eat that porridge. I think you are light-headed," Grandma said.

"Will I have time to finish the shirt? I thought I was going home tomorrow."

He shook his head. "No. You'll have to stay longer than that. This is serious business, Maria. "

"What will you tell Miss James and my classmates?"

"Miss James knows the whole story. She is going to tell your classmates that Anna was upset because she has to move, and you followed her to comfort her. In addition, you have an elderly maiden aunt in Boston who is ill, and we sent you up there to help her."

"What about Lizzie and Diana and Simon? What did you tell them?"

"The same story. Now they're all excited about having an auntie they didn't know about in Boston. They want to meet her."

Maria finally took a sip of tea. "I can hear them now, pestering Mama. Are Anna and her mother safe?"

"Very safe."

"Where are they?"

"I can't tell you that. I'm not sure myself."

Grandma rolled her eyes at Maria. "Didn't I already say so? If everyone knew where the safe houses were, they wouldn't be safe."

"Well, then, can I come to the meeting this Saturday? It's only down the street."

Papa and Grandma glanced at each other; both said no at the same time.

"I don't understand why I can't go to the meeting. The church is just a few doors away."

"Maria, it's still dangerous," Grandma said.

"There's somebody out there who had a very good look

at you and Anna both," said Papa. "These slave-catchers make a good living searching for runaways all over the city." He stood up. "All kinds of people come to our public meetings, and not all of them are good abolitionists, either."

Papa walked toward the door, and Maria followed him. "Anyone seeing you or Anna will remember you. You have to stay hidden until this thing dies down."

"But, Papa . . ."

"Now, don't be hardheaded, and don't pester your grandmother." His eyes weren't so gentle now.

Maria sighed. *I should be there,* she thought, *speaking for Anna, telling how she needed money and that I tried to start a sewing circle to raise money for her.* "Papa, I won't pester. Will you and Moosa come on Saturday to see me after the meeting?"

Even though he still looked angry, he kissed her on the forehead. "Yes, we'll be here."

"And on Sunday, too?"

"No. Because we don't want the children to know you're here. And in case anyone is nosing around the school, asking questions."

"I know you miss your family." Grandma's eyes appeared weak and tired as she looked at Maria.

Maria was afraid she had hurt her feelings. "You're my family, and I love being here with you, Grandma, but I just . . ."

"I understand, but it has to be this way for a while," Grandma said.

* * *

All Saturday evening, Maria listened for the sound of Papa's wagon. She hoped they'd come and not disappoint her, though as far as she could remember, Papa had never disappointed her. While Grandma sweetened the whole house with the scent of the gingerbread she was baking, Maria sat in the kitchen with her and worked on her shirt, stitch by annoying stitch. She tried not to think about Anna and the failed sewing circle, and wondered what the girls were doing this Saturday night.

Suddenly, she heard the wagon and put down her sewing.

When Papa and Moosa walked in, life seemed almost normal again.

Moosa and Maria went to talk in the sitting room, while Papa and Grandma drank tea in the kitchen. Moosa plopped down in Grandma's rocking chair, and Maria sat across from him on the sofa that was as big, saggy, and comfortable as their sofa at home.

"The man came by the school again, but Headmaster Clark chased him off. And so he threatened to come back with the marshal. We've been keeping watch around the school."

"Who?"

"Mr. Francis, Mr. Davis, me, Papa, and all of the men of Cedar Lane. We take turns."

"All those people know?"

"Of course. Everyone hates slave-catchers."

She gazed at Grandma's pipe, sitting on the fireplace mantel. "What about the children?"

"They ask about you every day. We can't say your name

in front of Simon, because he begins to cry, but Lizzie is suspicious. She keeps asking Mama why we never heard about this aunt before."

"Oh, my poor baby brother. I just want to hold him. Lizzie is the smartest one of us all, Moosa. She *would* be suspicious."

Moosa nodded. "I have some news. The older girls at school know the whole story, too."

"How, Moosa? Who told them?"

"The rumors. Everyone on Cedar Lane was searching for you and Anna that night. And everyone heard that a stranger had been lurking about, asking for a girl from the school. Little Miss figured it out for herself. Sarah, Naomi, all of the older girls know. But they're not breathing a word, especially to the younger children."

Maria leaned toward Moosa. "I betrayed Anna. That Little Miss is such a clack tongue and . . ."

Moosa held up his hand and gazed at her with Papa's intense eyes. "No, Maria. Little Miss confided in me and said she guessed about Anna, and she figured out why you wanted the circle to help her. She told me that she's gotten every girl in the school to join. Since school will be over next month, Miss James is letting them sew all day. Elizabeth and Diana are at Little Miss's house tonight for the sewing circle."

Maria looked doubtful. "Is that really true? All of the girls joined the circle?"

"That's what Elizabeth said. See what you've started? I have a new name for you. I'm calling you Little Truth."

* * *

Maria spent the quiet days with her beloved grandmother, looking forward to the time when she could go home. On Sundays, the aunts, uncles, and cousins visited, and they all ate together. It wasn't too different from her usual Sundays with Grandma Isabella. Though the uncles and aunts knew what had happened, the cousins asked why Elizabeth, Diana, and Simon weren't there. Maria kept her promise and didn't pester her grandmother. And one evening, as she sat in the kitchen while Grandma baked gingerbread, she quietly and without fanfare finished the shirt.

When Moosa and Papa came that Saturday evening, she gave it to them so that Elizabeth could take it to school. Moosa would tell Elizabeth that Maria had sent the shirt by post.

At least she wouldn't have to stand in front of Miss James and be told that the shirt was "haphazard."

And for the many days she was with Grandma Isabella, the name Little Truth always brought her comfort.

Papa and Moosa visited her every Saturday after the meeting. "The girls are still mad for sewing, Maria," Moosa informed her on one of his visits.

And each time he and Papa came to Grandma's house, Maria would ask, "When do you think I can go home?"

"When Papa thinks it's safe, Little Truth."

Finally, a few weeks later, Papa said that it was safe for Maria to return home. "The society will see to it that the money is paid for Anna's freedom."

"Did they pay the money yet? Is she free? When can I see her?"

"Calm down, Maria. I don't have all the answers now. But you can return home. There won't be any more slave-hunters snooping around."

CHAPTER 31

Spring Frolic

Even before they reached the school, Maria smelled the barbecue. She could see, in her mind's eye, Mr. Davis and Mr. Francis clearing out the pit behind the church and burning wood until it turned into coals. Then they'd skewer a whole pig on a long pole, hang it across the pit, and stay there for most of the day, slowly turning the pig. Maria's mouth watered. This was their spring-frolic treat.

Her heart raced when Uncle George steered the horses and wagon to a spot behind Zion Church. Grandma sat next to him in the front of the wagon. She turned around. "Well, Maria, you're finally home."

The younger cousins sat in the back of the wagon with Maria, squirming and wiggling with excitement. When she saw the white spires of Zion Church, she wanted to leap out of the wagon before Uncle George came to a full stop.

As they had been doing for the past ten years, the children of Colored School Number Three held their spring festival on the second Saturday in May.

The elms, beeches, black walnut, and sugar maple trees surrounding them were no longer bare, but in full leafy dress. The hills were decorated with green vines and bushes and fragrant with pink honeysuckle vines.

"God has made a beautiful day for us," Grandma said as Maria helped her climb out of the wagon. The cousins jumped out and scrambled toward the picnic tables and the other children. Maria hooked arms with Grandma, and then she spotted Papa, Moosa, and the other men, cleaning the picnic tables.

"Go on, Maria, I'll be fine, " Grandma said.

As Maria ran toward them, she suddenly heard a loud screech and saw Diana tearing over in her direction, a basket filled with biscuits swinging dangerously on her arm.

"Maria, Maria!"

Several birds flew out of a maple tree, and people looked in the direction of the commotion. Maria bent down and hugged her sister tightly. Simon ran up and fell and got up again before leaping into Maria's arms. Suddenly she was surrounded by them all. Mama held her close, and Maria almost cried when she smelled her familiar rose water scent. Elizabeth had to push between Little Miss and Sarah to reach her sister.

"Maria, come and see what we did while you were

gone!" Little Miss pulled on her arm as people continued to greet her. Byron jumped up and down and waved. The Magpie, carrying a platter of deviled oysters, chattered excitedly. "Oh, Maria, we're so glad you're home."

With Diana, Elizabeth, and Simon sticking to her like glue, Maria let Little Miss lead her to the large elm tree where the path to the school grounds ended. "I made the sign, Maria, and your brother tacked it on to the tree." Maria had never seen Little Miss so excited. The sign read: STITCHING FOR FREEDOM.

The girls had placed squares of paper with the prices on them on all of the articles. Elizabeth, Sarah, Little Miss, and the rest of the girls stood proudly behind two tables filled with the items they'd made.

Maria looked with amazement at the dresses, shawls, beaded purses, socks, samplers, skirts, shirts, pincushions, and at Amy's dolls—an African doll with a head wrap and earrings made out of gold-colored paper and a Spanish doll in a red-and-white dress with more ruffles than there were on Diana's pantalets. One item caught her eye, and she covered her mouth with her hand. "My shirt!" she said. "You included my shirt."

"Miss James said we should include it so that you'd have something to sell, too," Elizabeth said.

Maria shook her head. "You all made so many things. They're beautiful." She looked at them all, but her gaze lingered a bit longer on Little Miss. "Thank you for keeping the circle." She said.

No sooner had she said that than Miss James glided

over to her with outstretched arms. "Maria, I am so happy to see you. Welcome home."

Maria had never thought she'd ever be gathered up in Miss James's arms and never thought she'd be so happy to see her teacher. All she could think to say was, "My shirt was good?"

Miss James looked amused. "Well, Maria, the corners of your hem are very neat. No knots making it look sloppy. I saw a few stitches not quite straight in the right seam, but all in all you've done a decent piece of work." She fingered one of the buttonholes. "These buttonholes are perfect. I knew you could do it; that's why I insisted that you make it over. It's plain and simple and sturdy. That's all I ask for. You will be in the Class of Merit, and a monitor next school term."

The girls laughed and clapped, and Maria said, "Thank you, Miss James. Now I can be the official reader for the sewing circle."

Miss James smiled and shook her head. "You are still Maria."

Maria stepped behind the table, with Elizabeth and Diana on either side of her.

"How's our auntie?" Diana asked.

"Yes, is she better now?" Elizabeth asked.

"I'll tell you later," she said, making space for Simon, who stayed by her side also, until he saw several of his friends playing leapfrog.

Maria could not stop smiling as people continued to greet her. She forgot about looking around for suspicious strangers lurking. Maybe it was the smell of barbecue, but people in the neighborhood came also, even some from down the hill. But on this beautiful morning no one looked suspicious to Maria.

As more people strolled into the yard, Maria did find herself looking for Anna's tall figure. She couldn't stop thinking how nice it would have been if Anna were there. Perhaps it would soon be safe for her to come out of hiding, too, now. Then she remembered. Anna was still not free. Maria stayed behind the tables helping the girls sell as much as they could. Whenever someone looked at the items and then started to walk away without buying anything, Maria would pick up a doll or shirt and say, "Did you see this?"

The girls stood behind the tables waiting for customers, as the other children wasted no time in organizing games. Byron and his friends started a game of Touch, Moosa and a group of older boys went to the far end of the yard to play ball, Diana and her friends played I Spy, and Simon and his little friends chased each other about playing tag. Dukie and several other neighborhood dogs ran with the little ones.

The women began to put the food on the tables while the men helped the boys with the games or advised Mr. Francis and Mr. Davis on the barbecuing. Papa was among the barbecue advisers. By noon the food was ready.

Reverend Arlington said a prayer before they ate.

"Lord, we thank you for this beautiful day and for all

of your blessings. We know that everything comes from you, Lord, and without your grace and love we would have nothing. You are the author of all of our plans. Amen."

After the reverend ate, he left, and Mr. Francis's brother took out his fiddle and played and the children began to dance. Maria clapped and stayed behind the table.

The dancers formed two lines, men facing the women. Byron came over to Maria and bowed. "Maria, would you get in the line and dance with me?"

She giggled. "You have to grow taller."

"Come on, Maria, dance with me."

Emily took Maria's place behind the table while Maria danced with Byron. She saw Mama and Papa dancing as well, and they rarely danced. The Magpie moved her feet almost as quickly as Diana.

Maria clapped and laughed as she watched Diana try to imitate the men she'd seen in front of the saloon. Her little sister twirled and crossed her ankles, white pantalets flashing. Then Mr. Francis's brother played a very popular song that everyone could sing.

Maria almost missed a step when she saw Miss James and Headmaster Clark join the dance. Moosa and Little Miss danced together, too, and she was surprised. He wasn't such a good dancer. But on this day, it didn't seem to matter. Everything was good.

Maria started folding the articles that were left over, among them her shirt and Amy's Spanish doll. As Maria watched Little Miss carefully counting the money, she felt she had to say something to her. "Amelia, thank you for everything."

Little Miss stopped counting. "I told you it's okay to call me Little Miss. And what are you thanking me for?"

"For getting the girls to join the circle. Moosa told me."

Little Miss resumed counting. "But it was the best idea that anyone ever had. And this turned out to be the best frolic we've ever had."

Maria nodded as she looked toward the western sky. The setting sun had painted lavender streaks across the heavens. Neither Maria nor Little Miss said anything about Anna. They didn't have to. "Thank you, Little Miss."

Little Miss grinned. "Even though there are some articles left, we made the huge sum of fifty dollars," she announced. Maria laughed excitedly and exchanged hugs with the others, but she couldn't stop thinking, *We need five hundred dollars for Anna.*

The shadows were deepening as they walked back up the hill after cleaning up. Papa strolled next to her. "Maria, you and the girls should be proud. You've raised a lot of money."

"They did, Papa, not me."

"If it wasn't for you nothing would have been raised."

"But it's not enough to free Anna."

"Every penny helps the cause."

"Anna is the cause, Papa." Suddenly, an idea came to her. If only he and Mama would agree to it.

"Papa, can I go downtown with you to the stores and see if I can sell the rest of the articles?"

She listened to the sounds of children laughing and people saying good-bye to one another as they entered their houses along Cedar Lane, and waited for him to say no.

CHAPTER 32

A PERFECT DAY, ALMOST

T HE MONDAY MORNING after the spring frolic, Maria had to pinch herself as she sat next to Papa in the horse and wagon clomping down the Bowery. Mama and Papa had let her skip school, since this was the last week. Mama had agreed with her. "It would be nice to sell every-thing," she'd said, "but, Solomon, that's so common to have Maria going in and out of those stores."

"She's with me," Papa replied, "and she is a smart young lady. She has to know what the world is like. She's only common if she makes herself that way."

This was the first time Papa had ever taken her to the various stores he dealt with. "These are not places for a young lady like you," he'd said whenever she had asked to go with him and Moosa.

The wagon crawled down the narrow street packed

with vendors selling apples, potatoes, onions, carrots, candlesticks, peanuts, candy, utensils, and almost anything else that could be put in a handcart. Ragpickers and children selling newspapers made up part of the crowd. She was reminded of the day she and Anna had walked down those streets.

As they rode along the Bowery toward Chatham Square, the vendors practically blocked their way. Some of the men were calling out, "Glass put in, glass put in."

"What glass are they talking about? They all sound like Farmer Gruner."

"They put glass in windows, and maybe they sound a little like him. They come from the same part of Germany, I suppose."

Besides the glaziers, there were other men and a few women peddling fish. Maria was fascinated by their cries and their accents. "Fresh shad!" one man cried as he boldly stood in the middle of the street, with wagons and horses moving around him. Another man cried, "Buy my tasty clams today, they always hail from Rockaway."

The wagon moved slowly through the crowded street. A man came up to them. "Sir, I have the sweetest and best buttermilk this side of the Bowery." He carried two large pails.

Papa smiled. "I have buttermilk, too. My wife makes the best."

"Do you need any straw, then?"

"No, sir," Papa said. "I have all the straw I need."

Maria looked back at the man as they moved on slowly. "Papa, that's funny. He's selling buttermilk, like you."

"That's what the colored down here mostly sell on the street. Buttermilk and straw. Now, some colored own dance halls and oyster bars and restaurants."

When they turned the corner on Mott Street they saw many small secondhand shops lined up alongside one another like soldiers. Some of them were junk shops, and some had clothing.

Maria's father stopped at a tidy-looking store with some of the clothing displayed outside on a line hanging in the front of the store. "Well, Maria, this is our first stop. Mr. Stanley is one of my best customers, but you never say yes to the first offer. Except for the buttermilk. I have a set price on that."

Papa took a pail of buttermilk from the wagon and carefully covered the rest, piling hay on top of it. He handed her the pail. "I can't let this buttermilk show. It will be stolen as soon as we turn our backs."

Papa handed Maria the large basket in which the sewing-circle articles were kept, and she followed her father into the shop. She wondered what her mother would have said about all of these store-bought clothes. Men's coats and suits were hung neatly on one rack and women's dresses on another. Children's clothing—boys' on one side and girls' on the other—hung in the front. Shoes were lined up on shelves. Many were so worn they looked as though they couldn't bear another step. But everything had been cleaned, mended, and pressed.

A thin older man with a thick mustache came out of the back of the store when they walked in. "Oh, Solomon, my friend," he said.

He spoke to Papa, but stared at Maria. "And who is this with you?"

"This is Maria, my daughter. Maria, Mr. Stanley."

"So you're showing her the business?"

"No. She won't be doing this kind of work. She'll be a schoolteacher someday."

I will? Maria thought.

"That's very nice." Mr. Stanley adjusted his glasses and looked at the basket. Papa motioned for Maria to rest it on the counter. "So, what do you have there?" asked Mr. Stanley.

"Some special items that my daughter's sewing circle made." Solomon opened the basket.

Mr. Stanley picked up one of Emily's beaded purses. "Okay, so what do you want to trade for this?"

"No trade today. I'm selling."

"Solomon, you're killing me here." He shrugged his shoulders. "You and I, we trade. I have no money to buy anything."

"That's a well-made bag, Mr. Stanley. You don't have anything like that in this store."

"Because this is a store for poor people, Solomon. The people who come in here would never want such a bag." He pointed to the shelves. "These people want shoes, not fancy purses. They don't even have money to put in a purse."

"You have daughters and a wife. Maybe they would like a nice purse like this one." Papa continued to hold the purse in front of Mr. Stanley.

"If I buy them fancy pocketbooks and purses, then I won't have any money for them to put in them." He took the purse from Papa, opened it, and pulled on the handle. "So, how much do you want for this?"

"Three dollars," Papa said.

"Three dollars! Why have you come here to rob me like this on a Monday morning? Solomon, this is not Fifth Avenue."

Maria almost gasped. *Such a lot of money,* she thought.

"Look at the workmanship, Mr. Stanley. This isn't something thrown together in a factory. This was made with love and care."

"Solomon, I'm a loving and caring man, but this much love and care I can't afford."

Maria covered her mouth so that she didn't giggle out loud. She liked the way Mr. Stanley talked.

"What can you afford, Mr. Stanley?"

"Nothing. I can't afford nothing. This is a secondhand store. Do you think people with money come in here to buy?"

"Sometimes people will fool you. Sometimes a woman might want something special that perhaps she can't afford, so suppose I sold this bag to you for two dollars and fifty cents?"

Mr. Stanley sat down and rubbed his forehead. "I'm going to faint, Solomon. You're giving me such a time. One dollar for the bag."

"Oh, no, my daughter's friend worked too hard on this. This is fine work, and you know it. Two dollars."

"Where are my smelling salts? Oh, my, you drive a hard bargain. One twenty-five."

"Mr. Stanley, now I need smelling salts. But I like you, so I'll give it to you for a dollar fifty. Now, I have another bag that's similar. If you buy both, I'll give you the second bag for a dollar." Papa went into the chest again. "Now, look here. I'll throw in this beautiful shawl for just a dollar also." In the end Mr. Stanley bought all three items.

Papa wiped his forehead with a handkerchief when they left the store. "Now, see, you received your first lesson in successful selling."

"But you asked for three dollars for the purse and only got one dollar and fifty cents."

"A dollar fifty is what I wanted for the purse, but if I had said that price at first, then he would've gone lower. You have to bargain out here in order to get your price." Papa helped her into the wagon. "You have to make people feel they're getting something extra, too. Selling Mr. Stanley two bags and a shawl was good. We've already made three fifty, and the day has just begun."

"But I'm tired already. Will the other store owners be like him?"

"More or less."

They rode past a couple of pawnshops and more junk shops. "I don't deal with those, because they take stolen goods. If I trade with them, then I may be buying stolen property."

For the rest of the morning, Papa delivered the buttermilk to his regular customers on Mott Street and managed to sell three more shawls, two skirts, some socks and handkerchiefs, and Maria's shirt, which he sold for fifty cents, though he had tried to get a dollar for it. The only article left was Amy's doll.

They joked about it as they headed downtown to Wall Street. "I should be ashamed that my shirt only fetched fifty cents. But I'm glad to see it gone," she grinned. "That shirt caused me a lot of trouble. I would have given it to that shopkeeper for nothing."

Papa smiled. "It fetched something, so that means it was worth something. Anyway, Maria, you've made twenty-five dollars more for the abolitionists—a total of seventy-five dollars. You and the sewing-circle girls should be proud of what you've done."

Maria wanted to ask Papa about Anna, but didn't want to make him angry. They'd been having a fine time, and she didn't want to spoil it. They rode down Baxter Street, and she laughed at the organ-grinders and their dancing and cavorting monkeys.

"I have several pails of buttermilk to deliver to Mr. Downing," said Papa. "He's a colored man and has a catering house on Wall Street. He's another one of my best customers." They reached Wall Street, turned the corner on Broad Street, parking the horse and wagon in the back of a two-story brick building. They climbed out of the wagon, and Papa handed her two pails. "Mr. Downing is a member of the society, Maria. He's a generous man and helps us all of the time."

"Papa, do you think one day I'll be able to go to the meeting with you and Moosa?"

Papa took two more pails out of the wagon. "I guess you can. But you'll be busy with the sewing circle on Saturdays now."

"The circle is over now, Papa. School is over, and Anna is gone."

"What does Anna have to do with it?"

"Papa, I started it to raise money to help her."

He stared at his daughter as if he were finally understanding her. "Maria, that was a lot of money you and the girls raised. This money will be a real help to the abolitionists."

"But it won't free Anna," Maria said as they walked to the entrance of the restaurant.

He stopped before they entered. "Don't be so sure of that, Maria. You know, I think your mother has forgiven you, even though she still talks about how foolhardy you were to walk downtown. But you can come to the meeting on Saturday when we turn in the money. I want you present it to the society."

Maria smiled so widely her face felt as if it would crack. "Oh, Papa, Papa, thank you. Thank you so much."

They entered a large kitchen. Great pots and pans

hung everywhere, and a large cast-iron frying pan with feet stood on the coals in the tremendous hearth. A spit, the length of the hearth, held two chickens. There were large kettles and three of the biggest ovens she had ever seen for baking breads and pies. There were so many delicious scents that she couldn't distinguish any one in particular, except for the smell of bread and the roasting chickens.

A man who seemed to be the main chef stood in the middle of the room directing the other cooks and a couple of young women who washed pans in a large tub. He walked over to them, and another man took the pails from Papa and Maria.

"Hello, Solomon."

"Hello, Mr. Downing." The two men shook hands.

"I see you've brought the buttermilk, and who is this young lady?"

Papa put his arm around Maria's shoulder. "This is my daughter. She started a sewing circle to raise money for the society."

"Wonderful, wonderful." The man stared at Maria. "We need more young people like you. Did you bring something to sell?"

"No, we sold everything, Mr. Downing," Papa said.

Maria started to mention the doll, but it seemed as though it were too small an item.

Mr. Downing led Papa and Maria to another room. "Have lunch here."

Papa shook his head. "Sir, I don't want to impose on . . ."

"No. I insist you and your lovely daughter have lunch here."

The smaller and cooler room was just off the main kitchen, where Mr. Downing's employees ate. There were a small fireplace with several chairs around it and a long table. Three other people sat around the table eating.

Everyone knew Papa. As he and Maria sat down, he introduced her to the others. "This is my daughter, who started a sewing circle to raise money for the abolitionist cause."

How proud she felt to be there, like a grown-up, drinking the delicious turtle soup, having lunch with Papa. A thought suddenly came to her. "Papa," she said softly, "why are you telling everyone here about raising money for the abolitionists? You didn't tell any of the shopkeepers."

"A lot of people think the abolitionists are crazy troublemakers. So it was better not to say anything. Here, we are among colored people. It's different."

Maria felt happy and satisfied as they rode back home. For a moment she pushed the things that bothered her way back in a corner of her mind. *I can't wait to tell Mama and everyone what a wonderful day we had*, she thought. She enjoyed looking at the familiar sights on the way uptown. When she saw the Crystal Palace at Fortieth Street, she remembered for some reason that the only article they hadn't sold was Amy's doll. They'd soon be passing the Colored Orphan Asylum at Forty-fourth Street.

She waved as she always did when they passed the asylum, and the children waved back, except for one little girl about three years old who sat by herself, away from the others. Maria tapped her father on his arm. "Papa, can we stop?"

"What? Why?"

"I want to give the doll that's left to that little girl. She looks so sad, staring at her feet."

"Well, I guess it's okay to do that. But one of the bigger children might take it away from her. See if there's an older boy or girl who will look out for her."

He stopped the wagon, and Maria climbed out and walked the few feet to the yard where the children played. She saw a girl who seemed to be too old to play with dolls and called her to her. "Would you give this to that girl over there and make sure no one takes it from her?"

"Yes, ma'am," the girl said, sounding like Anna. She went over and gave the doll to the child and then pointed to Maria, still standing outside the fence. The little girl's smile was wide and bright as she hugged the doll. Maria waved to her as she walked back to the wagon.

"Well, Maria, you made that little girl happy."

"I hope no one takes the doll."

"Someone might. It's a cruel world sometimes. But that was a kind thing you did, and I don't think that girl will ever forget it."

When they arrived uptown and started up the hill toward Cedar Lane, Maria thought how different it was from the crowded and muddy streets downtown. They passed Zion Church and the school. Why would she ever want to live anywhere else?

No sooner had she had that thought than they walked into Mama's store, and the perfect day with Papa changed instantly.

CHAPTER 33

CEDAR LANE

MARIA KNEW THAT something was wrong. When she and Papa entered the store, it was crowded. The Magpie was the first person she saw, and then Byron's mother. Even Mrs. Davis, Little Miss's mother, who rarely came to the store, was there, along with Farmer Gruner and Moosa. Mama was holding a letter, and Maria noticed that her eyes looked sad and lacked their usual sparkle. No one was smiling.

"Solomon, we finally have news from the city," Mama said. She handed Papa the letter. "They're taking all of the property here, too. Everything. Our homes, the church, the school. Everything."

Papa took the letter. "We all knew that this might happen," he said solemnly. "So now we have to have go to the other plan."

Maria wondered how everything could be so perfect one moment and then miserable the next. But for the first time in her life she felt sorry for Mrs. Hamilton and vowed never to call her the Magpie again. Looking frightened as she wrung her hands, she cried, "My dear, dead husband worked so hard to give me this piece of house and lot. This is all that I own in this world."

Mama turned to Maria. "Go and help your brother with his reading. He missed you today."

As she walked away, Maria heard Mama consoling Mrs. Hamilton. Would things ever be normal again? Mama called her as she was about to walk down the short hallway connecting the store to the house. "Maria, don't say anything to the children yet."

"Yes, Mama."

As soon as she entered the kitchen, Elizabeth and Diana pounced on her.

"Maria, why are so many people in the store?" Elizabeth asked.

"And what are they talking about?" Diana chimed in.

Simon pulled Maria's dress. "It's time for my lesson."

She patted him on his head. "Get your books." Then she turned to Elizabeth and Diana. "Mama and Papa will tell us when they come in."

"They tell you and Moosa everything. It's about the house, isn't it?" Elizabeth's worry lines furrowed her forehead.

"Lizzie, they don't tell me everything." Maria and Elizabeth both sat down at the table. Simon was busy thumbing through his reader, and he ignored his sisters. Maria noticed Diana heading down the hallway toward the store.

"Come back here and help Lizzie with the supper," Maria ordered.

Diana kept walking as if she hadn't heard her.

Elizabeth carefully sliced a carrot. "So, how was your day with Papa?" she asked. Her expression was sour—not like that of the usually sweet Elizabeth.

"We sold everything and made twenty-five dollars."

Simon found his lesson and began to read the vocabulary words for the story. "*Kate, dear, milk, old, likes, cow, no, be, out, grass, drink, gives.* Did I get all of the words right, Maria?"

"Yes, perfect."

Diana ran back and forth between the store and the kitchen, but when she came back for the third time, her face was somber.

"What happened to you?" Elizabeth asked.

Diana's bright eyes filled with tears. "Papa shouted at me to stay in the house."

"I told you to keep out of their business," Maria said.

"Why are all of those people in Mama's store? You want to know too, Lizzie, don't you?" Diana asked.

Elizabeth picked up a potato from the bowl on the table and took a knife and handed them both to Diana. "Maria says that Mama and Papa will tell us."

As Maria helped Simon with his lessons, she could hear the little bells tinkling every time someone opened and closed the door to the store. She found it hard to concentrate on Simon as she tried to imagine not living on Cedar Lane. Neither petitions nor prayers seemed to work.

It wasn't until evening, after they'd eaten and cleared the table and washed the dishes, that Papa called all of them into the sitting room. Maria tried to swallow the lump in her throat and be brave.

"Children, I have something to tell you," said Papa. "We'll be moving from Cedar Lane. I have tried to buy property nearby, but it is too dear, and many landowners won't sell to colored. I even inquired about land in the village of Flushing. I was told that I could work on farms, but there was no land for sale, or that I could work the land for a certain number of years and then buy." He shook his head.

"That's no bargain," Moosa said. "You could work for ten or twenty years and never get any land."

"I know, and that's why I've made the decision to move to Kansas."

Moosa sat up. "Kansas? We should be going all the way west, to California, Papa."

"You are right, son; the only place to get any kind of land is in the territories, but I'm not going on a fool's errand."

Maria looked from her father to her brother. They were so much alike.

"You mean, looking for gold?" Moosa asked.

"Yes." Papa turned his gaze toward the rest of his

family. "We will go to Kansas. A small group of abolitionists from Massachusetts already have a settlement there, and I am told that there is a good amount of available land. We'll have more than just a house and two little plots." His eyes rested on Mama, as if he wanted to make sure she heard what he was saying, as if they had discussed this before and now he were trying to convince her. "This may be our last chance for land. There is none to be had here. Catalina, your own mother is always telling stories about your family losing land and property in the city."

Mama's eyes were still sad and spiritless. "That was over one hundred years ago. She's just repeating stories she heard when she was a girl," she said.

Maria was amazed at the way happiness came and went so quickly. The other children, including Elizabeth, seemed confused. "Are we leaving tomorrow?" Diana asked. "Where are we going?"

"Where are we going?" Simon repeated.

"We're not going anywhere for a while," Papa said.

Moosa, coming out of his own thoughts, said, "I want to go to California. There's land and gold. I've never heard of anything in Kansas."

Papa's gaze appeared weary and angry all at once. "Just because you've never heard of something doesn't mean it doesn't exist. Who are you? A boy with foolish ideas." His voice boomed. "You need to let go of childish dreams and think on serious things. There's no gold anymore in California. Most of the people who went there barely returned with the shirts on their backs."

Moosa stood up. "It makes no sense to go just part of the way to a settlement. What will we do there?"

"We can get land. Land is wealth. But I want you to continue with your schooling. Go to that Oberlin College in Ohio that accepts colored."

"I can't use that education after I get it." Moosa's voice trembled slightly, but he glared back at his father. "I learned navigation in school, top student in my class, but I can't get work as a navigator."

"So, you want to navigate a boat across the desert to a gold mine? Look at Dr. Jones. You could be like him."

Moosa said nothing more.

Maria felt sorry for him and for herself. Her head throbbed.

Mama continued to knit furiously.

Papa said, "Now let's talk about something good. Maria, tell them what you did today, and don't leave out the part about giving the little girl a doll."

So Maria recounted her day with Papa.

"See," Papa said, "this is something to rejoice over. That money will help someone. Because this has happened to us doesn't mean that we can't continue to do what we must. Or laugh, even. What do I always tell you children?" He stared at each one of them, and they looked back at him with blank faces.

Then Elizabeth remembered. "As long as we're together, we're home."

CHAPTER 34

THE MEETING

MARIA HEARD SIMON'S cries as she sat in the wagon waiting for Moosa to climb in. Simon and Mama were the only two not going to the meeting. "That poor baby is so hurt," Papa said.

"That's because Diana is going, too. That hurts him more than anything else," Elizabeth said, turning to Diana. "You should have told him we were going to school. He wouldn't know the difference."

Moosa pulled the reins on the horse. "He knows the difference when he sees all of us getting in the cart. Our little brother isn't stupid."

Maria was excited and nervous at the same time. As they rode along, they picked up Sarah and Amy. Little Miss and the other girls were going to the meeting with their parents; there were thirty in all. Papa had joked with Maria that morning. "See what you've started?" he asked. "Almost everyone on Cedar Lane is going to the meeting."

Maria gazed at the warm orange glow cast by the setting sun over the trees and bushes as the wagon bumped over the ruts and holes on Cedar Lane. "I will miss this place," she said.

Sarah said, "We have to keep it in our minds and remember it exactly as it is."

Amy giggled. "I will never forget Examination Day, when Byron ripped his pants." They laughed loud and long as they talked of other moments at their school with their friends. Then Maria said, "I'll never forget the first time I saw Anna, sitting down front with the little ABCers."

"That was a sight," Sarah chuckled, "but I still miss her. No one could tell that crazy tail story as she could."

"You mean, tailypo. 'Give me back my tailypo,'" Diana shouted over the clanging wagon. And of course, Diana told it with growls and screams, and even Papa had to say, "Daughter, you'll cause Moosa to have an accident." Maria saw his shoulders rise and fall and knew that he was chuckling, too. She and the girls found something to laugh and smile about all the way downtown.

As soon as they entered the church, Maria recalled the time that she and Anna had been there looking for Miss Truth. Now the church was full. It wasn't long after they had entered the church that the rest of the girls arrived.

"I want you girls to sit in the front," Papa said. "One of you will present the money to the society. Decide among yourselves who's going to do it."

The girls stared at one another. Maria looked around for Grandma Isabella and saw her talking to several women. She wondered if Anna and her parents might show up. What a wonderful thing that would be!

"Come on, girls. You have to decide," Papa said.

Moosa, sitting between Maria and Elizabeth, cleared his throat. "I think Maria should do it."

Maria turned around. "Maria should do what?"

Little Miss looked up at Moosa with a smile on her face. "Your brother is right, Maria. You should present the money."

Diana crossed her legs. "I'll do it if Maria doesn't want to." Then she turned to Elizabeth. "What do I have to do?"

Elizabeth laughed and shushed her.

"No. I want Maria to do this, " Papa said.

"But Papa, Miss James said she'd be here. I think she should present the money. Or Little Miss—I mean, Amelia."

Papa shook his head. "You can do it, Maria."

Maria poked Moosa in the side. "You wait until we get home, Mister Moosa."

Moosa grinned. "Just give Dr. Jones the money and say where it's from, Maria. That's all. Oh, and say how much you raised."

The more crowded the church became, the louder

Maria's heart thumped. She had thought that only a few people came to the antislavery meetings. But now, even the balcony was getting crowded. She tried to calm her nerves, and she poked Moosa again; he grinned in response.

She had no idea how she'd find the nerve to stand up before so many people and talk.

Men and women and a few youngsters continued to enter the church. Diana's large eyes roved over the entire crowd. She kept pointing out to Elizabeth what the women were wearing. "Lizzie, that girl is wearing a pretty blue bolero jacket and bonnet to match. See over there?"

"Stop pointing," Elizabeth said. "That's rude."

The majority of the audience was black, but a good number of whites were sprinkled among them.

Maria tried to be calm. *I only have to say a few words,* she thought. As she observed people sitting in the pews, she wondered whether the whites would cause trouble and holler obscenities, as Mama had described in her stories about the riot. Those thoughts didn't help her nerves. So, she imagined Miss Truth, standing tall. She guessed that the whites were all abolitionists and antislavery people, too. She didn't think they were the hooligans and ruffians her mother always talked about.

A thin, distinguished-looking man with a full head of thick gray hair, contrasting with a dark brown complexion, stood before the audience. Suddenly the church was very quiet. Since it wasn't a church service, he didn't stand in the pulpit, but in front of the altar.

"Good evening, ladies and gentlemen. I am thrilled that so many of you have answered the call to this important meeting of the New York branch of the American Anti-Slavery Society."

"Moosa, who is he?" Maria whispered.

"He's the chairman of the society. Dr. George Jones. He's the only colored doctor in this city, as far as I know."

"He's the doctor Papa is always talking about?"

"Yes."

Dr. Jones cleared his throat and spoke in a deep, heavy tone. "As some of you may already know, we have saved yet another unfortunate caught in the snares of slavery."

For a moment, Maria thought he was talking about Anna.

"We have been able to free our brother, John Hamer. A word to your friends, Mr. Hamer."

A short brown man who reminded Maria of Anna's father walked to the front of the church, and Maria forgot her own discomfort. This was the man that Papa and Moosa had told her about. The one for whom Miss Truth had raised so much money.

His hands shook nervously, and he bowed his head slightly, thanking everyone. Maria thought that he sounded more nervous than she felt. She gazed around the church again, thinking how wonderful it would be if Anna and her parents spoke next, thanking the society for freeing Anna—if Anna had, in fact, been freed.

When Mr. Hamer finished talking, Dr. Jones returned to the front of the altar.

"And now, we have a very special presentation from our young people." He looked at all of the girls sitting before him. "Who is going to make the presentation?" All of the girls stared at Maria. Sarah leaned over Moosa, whispering, "Go on, Maria."

Maria tried to hold her head high, as Miss Truth would have. She walked slowly to the front of the church and felt all eyes on her. Inside, though, her stomach churned, and her voice came out in a little squeak as she stared at the smiling Dr. Jones.

"I . . . I . . . Good evening, Dr. Jones."

Dr. Jones continued to smile at her. "Don't be nervous, my child. Face the audience," he whispered.

She turned to the audience and instantly felt like running. She looked at Papa, who nodded reassuringly, and kept looking at him only. Clearing her throat, she found a better and louder voice. "On behalf of the girls' sewing circle called Stitching for Freedom, we present seventy-five dollars to the New York City Anti-Slavery Society."

Everyone murmured and then clapped loudly. Maria saw Miss James in the audience and spotted Mr. Downing, too. Grandma Isabella sat up proudly. She looked at all of the girls and found her real voice. "This money was raised by all of the girls in the sewing circle of Colored School Number Three. My papa helped us to sell, too."

She handed the money to Dr. Jones, and he turned to her.

"This money will help us to save another person," he

said. "All donations, as you know, go to help our brethren who are still in the chains of slavery." He pointed to the girls. "I want all of you young ladies to stand." The audience clapped, and the girls smiled proudly before sitting back down.

When Maria started to return to her seat, Dr. Jones stopped her and faced the audience. "You have no idea how much this donation helps us to continue our work here. We were without any funds. It took all of our money to obtain freedom for a young lady caught in the jaws of slavery."

Maria was afraid even to think it: was he referring to Anna?

Dr. Jones turned to Maria. "We would have had to close our doors for a while if we hadn't received this donation."

As Maria shook his hand, she smiled; she really wanted to twirl around the way Diana did when she was joyful.

Before she knew what was happening, she heard Dr. Jones say, "And here is the young lady and her family." Maria turned around and saw Anna, her mother, and her father, coming out of the door to the left of the altar. The same door Maria had banged on when she and Anna came to the church two months before.

The people in the church burst out in applause, and Anna and Maria embraced and cried and laughed. Diana ran to the front of the church to hug Anna, and the other girls followed. Dr. Jones quieted everyone. He turned to

Anna and her parents. "Young lady, would you like to say a word?"

Maria thought that Anna would stare at the ground and shake her head no. But, surrounded by Maria and the rest of the girls, she spoke up, faltering a little at first. "This is . . . this is . . . my best friend, who help to save me and my mother and father. She make me walk down here for help. When I want to stop, she still make me walk." She breathed heavily and lowered her face, then raised her head again. "Her grandma, Dr. Jones, Maria's papa, and all of you help us, too. I a free girl now. Thank you."

The sewing-circle girls all stood up and clapped for Anna, and everyone else followed suit.

As they walked out of the church, people were still congratulating Maria and the girls. The night was clear and warm, with a full moon lighting the churchyard. Maria and Anna managed to separate themselves from the crowd and had a moment to talk alone.

"Maria, you must promise never to tell, but you'll never guess where we stay all these months," Anna whispered.

"Where?"

"Right here. At the church."

Maria looked confused. "What do you mean?"

"They have two secret rooms under the regular basement. That's where we hide. They feed us and take care of us and send the money for my freedom. You bring me to the right place, Maria."

Maria and Anna embraced. Like Miss Truth, Maria felt tall within.

One year later

MARIA STOOD AT the top of the small hill and waited, as she did every Sunday morning. From that spot she could see the whole neighborhood—the shanties and the swamps, and, on very bright, clear days, the meadowlands of the Jones estate on Sixty-ninth Street.

The church bells rang nine times, and she looked toward Zion Church and Colored School Number Three. A few people had already started walking up the path that led to the church and school buildings.

Maria was fourteen years old today, but did not wonder why fourteen still felt like thirteen. She'd been feeling older, different, for some months now. Since the past fall she'd been a monitor and a member of the Class of Merit. She was also the assistant Sunday school teacher, helping Mrs. Ball.

Maria continued the sewing circle, and everyone, including Mama and Miss James, accepted the fact that Maria did not do needlework. She was, instead, the official reader for the circle.

Every Sunday, she left home early so that she could wait for Anna, in case she was able to come to church. Anna could no longer attend school, because she had to work.

"But I still practice my reading and writing. I read packages, boxes, pieces of paper, anything with words," she had told Maria.

Anna's family never came back to the shanty they'd been renting; they now lived in another shanty, farther downtown on Eighth Avenue. They made the five-mile trek to Zion Church whenever they could; Anna tried to get there every Sunday. And this was the most important one of all.

It was the last time Maria would see the spires of Zion Church, pointing to heaven, and the two square white buildings of Colored School Number Three. The Peters family would be traveling westward in a couple of days.

Maria gazed toward the church again and saw Miss James entering. She had secured a job as a governess for a wealthy family in the city. She gave all of the girls her new address and offered to keep track of theirs. If they moved around often, they were to write to her, and she would share their addresses with their fellow classmates. Mama had said, "Miss James will live as a white woman now. No colored teacher could get such a position." Maria still couldn't imagine that there would be no more Colored School Number Three and no more Miss James to be the teacher.

She looked toward the church again and saw Anna in her burgundy cloak walking up the path. When Anna reached her, by the outcropping of rock, Maria noticed that she held a package wrapped in brown paper.

Maria stared at her friend and was struck again by how much she changed every time she saw her. Her eyes were clear and bright, no longer clouded by the shadows of slavery.

"I was hoping you'd come this Sunday," Maria said.

Anna handed Maria the package. "I had to give you this so that you'd always remember."

Maria opened the package and took out a small quilt. "Oh, Anna, this is beautiful!" She ran her hand over the material, smiling in recognition. "You've created a picture of Cedar Lane!"

"Yes. There's the church and the school buildings. The school yard and the trees.

"Thank you so much, Anna. I'll keep this forever."

"I made one for myself, too. Remember, I start the quilt last year in the sewing circle?"

Maria nodded. "I remember. We're leaving tomorrow, but I'll write you as soon as we get to Kansas." She gazed at the quilt again. "And remember that if you move, or if I move, we'll tell Miss James. In that way, we won't lose one another."

"We'll always be friends," Anna said. "My father say that he want to get his own land. Maybe one day we come to Kansas, too."

"That would be a wonderful thing, Anna."

By fall, Zion Church, Colored School Number Three, and all of the homes on Cedar Lane and the surrounding area were torn down, disappearing without a trace. A magnificent park, Central Park, replaced them.

Most of the characters in *Home Is with Our Family* are fictional, but the New York City setting in the years 1855–56 is real. At the time this story takes place, New York City had a number of free black residents like the Peters family. (Slavery ended in New York in 1827.) Many were active in the abolitionist movement and participated in Underground Railroad activity. Thus, New York became a magnet for people escaping slavery in the South.

In 1853, the city of New York informed the public that an area from Fifty-ninth to One hundred and sixth streets, between Fifth and Eighth avenues, would be opened up as a public place for a "grand" park. The majority of New Yorkers at this time lived in lower Manhattan, and the area was overcrowded with people and industries. Living conditions were unsanitary, especially for the poorest residents, many of whom were European immigrants. City leaders recommended that a majestic park be built in upper Manhattan in order to create new neighborhoods for wealthy New Yorkers. However, there were already people living in the area that was proposed for what we know today as Central Park; about 1,600 people would be removed. Property owners were paid for their homes and lots, but many protested having to give up their property against their will and the meager compensation they received.

About 300 of the residents who lost their property lived in a neighborhood called Seneca Village (an area situated between Eighty-second and Eighty-ninth streets and Seventh and Eighth avenues). This is the community on which Cedar Lane is based. Most of the residents of Seneca Village were African American. By the 1840s, a few Irish and German immigrants were also a part of Seneca Village. The community had three churches: the African Union Methodist Church, the African Methodist Episcopal Zion Church, and All Angels' Church. All Angels' Church was attended by African Americans and German immigrants. There were also several cemeteries designated as "colored." In those years, schools as well as cemeteries in New York were segregated.

Zion Church and Colored School No. 3 are all based on real institutions in Seneca Village. Colored School No. 3 is modeled after the New York African Free School No. 2, founded in 1787 by the New York Manumission Society for free children of African descent. The curriculum and method of instruction covered in my story follow the teaching methods used in this school. St. Philip's Church, the church that Grandma Isabella attends, is based on St. Philip's Episcopal Church, the first African American Episcopal church in New York City, which was established in 1818 and quite active in the abolitionist movement. St. Philip's Episcopal Church is still a thriving parish in Harlem, in upper Manhattan.

All of the other city settings are real as well: the Five Points neighborhood, where Grandma Isabella lived; the streets that Maria and Anna ran through as they sought Sojourner Truth; the Colored Orphan Asylum; and some of the stores and industries mentioned in this story. All are based on actual places in New York City.

Several people mentioned in the story are based on historical figures as well. Sojourner Truth was a famous African American abolitionist, whose dates were roughly 1797–1883. Her real name was Isabella Baumfree. George T. Downing (1819–1903) was a well-known black caterer and businessman in New York City. He was also an abolitionist and activist. Dr. George Jones is based on Dr. James McCune Smith (1813–1865), the first African American to earn a medical degree. He had to attend the University of Glasgow in Scotland, because he was denied admission to the American universities to which he had applied.

I was inspired to write *Home Is with Our Family* when I first learned about the little known but fascinating history of Seneca Village.

For further information about Seneca Village, visit **www.centralpark.com/pages/history/seneca-village.html**.